Arrow pointing nowhere /

Large Print Dal
Daly, Elizabeth, b. 1878.
Arrow pointing nowhere

☝ W9-BUD-884

GAYLORD M

Arrow Pointing Nowhere

Also by Elizabeth Daly in
Thorndike Large Print ®

The House Without the Door
Nothing Can Rescue Me
Somewhere in the House
Unexpected Night

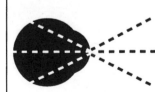

This Large Print Book carries the
Seal of Approval of N.A.V.H.

ARROW POINTING NOWHERE

Elizabeth Daly

Thorndike Press • Thorndike, Maine

Thorndike Large Print ® Americana Series edition published in 1993 by arrangement with Henry Holt and Company.

The tree indicium is a trademark of Thorndike Press.

Set in 16 pt. News Plantin by Heidi Saucier.

This book is printed on acid-free, high opacity paper.⊗

Library of Congress Cataloging-in-Publication Data

Daly, Elizabeth, b. 1878.
  Arrow pointing nowhere / Elizabeth Daly.
    p. cm.
  ISBN 1-56054-322-1 (alk. paper : lg. print)
  1. Gamadge, Henry (Fictitious character) —Fiction. 2. Book collectors —New York (N.Y.) —Fiction. 3. Large type books. I. Title.
  [PS3507.A4674A89 1993]
  813'.54—dc20   93-13143
                                                    CIP

Contents

1

GAMADGE HAS A LETTER

Schenck pushed the ball of crumpled paper across the table. "The trouble is," he said, "you don't get your mail."

Gamadge picked the thing up and smoothed it out. It proved to be a buff-colored envelope of good quality, addressed in neat typing to Blake Fenway, Esq., in the east seventies. A business address was printed in the upper left-hand corner: *J. Hall. Rare Books.* In the upper right-hand corner was a cancelled stamp; the postmark was dated January 29th.

After a glance at Schenck's face, which wore a peculiar smile, Gamadge turned the envelope over. It had been opened, and J. Hall's bill or circular removed; then, apparently, it had been crushed up and thrown into a waste basket. But first — or afterwards — somebody had printed Gamadge's name and address below the flap, untidily and with a pencil. Gamadge again looked enquiry at Schenck, looked down at the envelope, put two fingers into it, and withdrew a scrap of glazed white

7

paper. It looked as though it had been torn from the margin of a magazine. A pencilled line of print staggered across it:

RECOMMEND EARLY VISIT TO INSPECT INTERESTING CURIOSA. DISCRETION.

Gamadge studied this with surprise. Schenck permitted himself a cackling laugh, and his eyes glittered profanely. He was no longer the natty and ultrafashionable insurance investigator of other days; now a member in good standing of the Federal Bureau of Investigation, he wore the inconspicuous and sombre dress of the ordinary citizen. But at present he looked his foxiest.

Gamadge asked: "Who's been compromising me and J. Hall and Mr. Blake Fenway in this manner?"

"I don't know."

"Did you people get this out of an ash can? Did you intercede for me with your colleagues?"

"You're not far wrong." But Schenck's face lost its merriment as he extended a finger to point at the exhibits on the table: "There's proof that even a postman can be jounced out of his routine by sheer weight of accumulated evidence. But I don't know how many of those paper balls have been lost; the Fenway postman didn't notice any until a week ago yesterday, but he's seen five of them since. Never in the morning, always in the afternoon about three o'clock, when he makes his last delivery. Always in the same place, inside the railings, between the front steps and the service door. You know the old Fenway corner house?"

"Of course. It's completely detached, with grassplots between it and the street, and a big lawn to the south."

"And it fronts on the side street, and a ten-foot wall runs between it and the next house. They used to have their private stable behind the wall there, but the postman says that now it's a yard, running through to the garden and lawn. You go through a gate in the railing, along a flagged path, and through the service door, which is kept unlocked in the daytime. The grassplots around the house are nine or ten feet deep, and the railing is about four feet high. But when it reaches the lawn it shoots to ten feet, and there's a gate there too. Remember?"

"I remember."

"On Friday, January 22nd, the postman saw the first ball of paper; he was going along the flagged walk to the service door. It was lying about halfway between the door and the front steps, and about a yard inside the railing. A two-story bay window juts out above and be-

9

hind where it lay. He thought casually that the ashmen must have let it fall out of the can on their way to the street, and that the wind had blown it to the right. He also thought casually that it was funny the outdoor man had let it stay there; the Fenway place is kept as neat as a pin.

"There's no afternoon delivery on Saturday, so he didn't see the next ball until Monday. Tuesday he saw another, Wednesday he saw another. Thursday came the big storm, and he was a little late; but there was one of those balls sitting in the exact spot, with the snow beginning to cover it. If it had been there more than a minute or two it would have been covered, but that east wind we had kept blowing the snow off; it was good stiff paper like this one.

"He stood there with the storm whistling round his ears, and he wondered whether the things were there for him, and *only* for him; because the old Irishman that takes care of the place goes by clockwork, and cleans up the front of the premises at three-fifteen every afternoon; the postman met him at it when the delivery was late. Thursday was a near-blizzard, and perhaps the old fellow had quit entirely for the day. But on other days he'd be right along after the postman left, and he'd pick up any waste paper that happened to be lying around. Happened? The postman was beginning to think that there were too many coincidences happening around the Fenway house. He leaned over, bag and umbrella and all, and picked up the paper ball. It was blue."

"Not this one."

"No — there was a slight hitch in the proceedings; you can't expect too much cerebration from a postman making deliveries in a storm like that. It was nothing but an old envelope, business envelopes, he thinks from a bookstore."

Gamadge whistled.

"It seemed to be empty, and it was scrawled up with pencil marks; so he threw it away. He says he put it in the rubbish basket on the corner, but in a storm like that I shouldn't have bothered with rubbish baskets myself; he threw it away.

"Came yesterday, snow gone, sun out; postman walks through the gate in the railing at three o'clock sharp, and there's his ball of paper waiting for him; and this time he's sure it's for him. He grabs it up, but afterwards he looks up at the bow window. He had a look above it, to the top story. He wonders whether some child isn't trying to have some fun with him; his own kids like to throw things out of windows. But the curtains are all in place, layers of 'em; nobody ever looks out

11

of a window in a house like the Fenways'.

"He looks at the basement window under the bay. The basement's on ground level, windows barred; and they're all snowed up.

"He puts the envelope in his pocket, and goes through to the kitchen door, and delivers the mail. Mind you, he doesn't show what he's picked up to the maid that takes in the letters; he's pretty well convinced by now that the paper balls weren't meant to be seen by anybody but him, certainly not by anybody in the Fenway house.

"When he's on the street again he reads your address on the back of the envelope, and he finds the enclosure. They don't mean a thing to him, but he takes them along with him to his branch post office, and shows them to one of the sorters there, and tells the story. That," said Schenck, leaning slightly forward and rapping the edge of the table, "was what he was meant to do. A long shot, but did you ever know anything slicker?"

Gamadge met his eye. "Hardly ever."

"*Curiosa.* That's the magic word. The sorter didn't know what it implied, either; but he thought the whole thing was queer enough to be shown to the assistant postmaster. *He* knew what *curiosa* meant, all right, it's a word the post office is always on the lookout for, they're always watching for deleterious matter

12

sent through the mails.

"He was in a quandary, though; that scrap of paper there didn't look as if it had been meant to go through the mails, it looked like a jotting of a memorandum or rough draft of something J. Hall intended for his typist or his printer. Something to go into a circular or a special catalogue. And your name and address on the back of the envelope looked as if it had been meant for you. Well, he didn't know you, or J. Hall either; but he knew all about the Fenways. If Blake Fenway was going to be involved in this, the assistant post-master wasn't going to start the wheels turning until he'd had advice; especially after he heard that Thursday's envelope was blue. Another bookseller? He was in a fog. What he did was to call up a man he knows in our office here, and fix an appointment for the evening, and show him the exhibit.

"The man knows me, and knows I know you. He passed it along to me this morning, and here it is."

Gamadge was studying the scrap of paper again. He said: "Thanks."

"You wouldn't say it was all a mare's nest? Can J. Hall really have made that notation after all?"

"Most unlikely. I'm an old customer, and though I can't answer for Hall's morals, I know his ways. I don't think he ever in his life made a memorandum on a scrap like this, and I never saw him print anything. He writes a small, crabbed hand, and the printer can decipher it or go to the devil. His clerk doesn't make rough drafts; he types Hall's. And I should think yesterday's blue envelope settled that, anyway; the sender of this message only wanted a rare-book man, any rare-book man, as camouflage."

"In case one of the paper balls was found by the wrong party?"

"I'm afraid so."

"It does look as if somebody in the house was trying to communicate, and making heavy weather of it."

"It does. You and your colleague and the assistant postmaster and the sorter and the Fenway postman have all been very intelligent and discreet."

"I told them you'd probably be willing to look into it. But you're a busy man these days. I wasn't sure you'd have time for extra work."

"I always answer my letters."

"I guess it's meant for you, all right. The wonder is that it ever got to you."

"Well, I don't know; if J. Hall had been tackled, as he would have been in the ordinary course of things, he'd have tackled me — with ferocity."

"What do you make of it?" Schenck sat back to watch his friend, who was now inspecting the creased envelope.

"What anybody would. This was in a Fenway wastebasket; Fenway's undoubtedly a customer of J. Hall's, and since he received it so late in the month, it probably contained what mine contained; for I got one yesterday morning myself — a prestatement of next month's rarities. I must try to find my envelope; I'd like to answer this letter," said Gamadge, smiling, "and a Hall envelope would be the perfect envelope to use. This one was retrieved from the wastebasket by somebody who hadn't access to stationery, pens, or ink. It was addressed to me in a hurry and in the dark or under the edge of a table; certainly the enclosed message was written in those circumstances, or others not unlike them. The writer's eye wasn't on it.

"And in such circumstances print is even more difficult than handwriting. But the writer used print because he or she couldn't afford to be identified by handwriting. The writer hoped that if this were found, it would be attributed to J. Hall and thrown away."

"And the writer can't get out of the house and get to a mailbox. How about the finder tackling J. Hall about it?"

"Same result as the present one; J. Hall

would indignantly deny all knowledge of it, and pass it on to me."

"I suppose you'll see Hall, though?"

"Oh, yes. I'll have a word with him. He may be my hope — of meeting Mr. Fenway."

Schenck wrinkled up his forehead. "We're getting on; perhaps you don't know what we're heading into. You're making this out a kind of an affair that might be going on in some gangster's hideout; not too easy to pull off in some cellar or garage."

"I don't know what I can go by but the evidence."

"How about a hoax, or a servant with a grudge? Only the Fenways don't have servants with grudges; the postman says they stay till they're too old to work, and then they're pensioned off comfortably. How about a lunatic? The society editors I talked to this morning don't know anything about a lunatic, but the society editors don't know much about the Fenways, and that's a fact. You ought to hear them on the subject. The Fenways have a publicity phobia."

"That's in their favor."

"Yes, but the papers can hardly get vital statistics out of them, and when there's a wedding it's private, no pictures and no church ceremony, and when there's a funeral the deceased just slips away with two lines in the obituary column. The Fenways are about as obscure," said Schenck, "as the obelisk in Central Park, and they've been in New York a deuce of a lot longer; but they'd rather not be mentioned above a whisper."

"But there's never been any mystery about them, everybody knows their history. Old, distinguished, legal family, none better. Money acquired by judicious marriages, and the sale of prerevolutionary grants up the Hudson, and legal services to a distinguished clientele. The Fenways come from a very old English family, and always seem to have been more than well off. To use an old-fashioned mode of speech, they know everybody and go everywhere; which means that they know the chosen few and go where *they* go. I'm not less surprised than you are, Schenck, that a message like this one should have been thrown out of a Fenway window. Do you know who lives there now?"

"Blake Fenway, widower; his unmarried daughter; his only brother's widow, and — I think — her son. Her husband, Cort Fenway, died a long time ago; she always lived in Europe, but the war sent her back home. Oh — there's a cousin or something in the house, a Mr. Mott Fenway, elderly man; he's always lived there."

"Does Fenway still practise law?"

"Don't know. The firm is Fenway, Fenway and Chudley." Schenck wagged his head. "No wonder the assistant postmaster consulted another fellow before he did anything official about anything connected with that house! Why, there's never been any news about it, much less scandal! No, it's the family lunatic."

"Well: let's see what my orders are. I'm to go there and inspect something or somebody, perhaps try to get into touch with my client; but I must be discreet — I mustn't give the client away, or consult the police. I'm to go as soon as I can, I'm a week overdue."

"It's a man; women don't read rare-book catalogues and know about curiosa."

"Really, Schenck! Some women read everything they can lay their hands on. Don't you know any learned women?"

Schenck said he didn't.

"It would be easier to keep a woman under duress."

"But what kind of duress is it? The party has a certain amount of freedom — enough to throw paper balls out of a window. It's a corner house, facing a street and broadside-on to an avenue; even if the whole family's in the conspiracy, servants and all, your client ought to be able to make some kind of a row — yell fire or murder out of that window."

Gamadge said: "You forget the discretion clause in the message. My client doesn't seem to want a row."

Schenck rose. "It's a lunatic with a persecution mania. Watch your step, and a happy weekend."

Gamadge saw him into the little elevator, and then shouted down the stairs for his wife. She arrived in the company of Harold Bantz, once Gamadge's assistant, now sergeant of Marines and at home for repairs. Gamadge said that being torpedoed had mellowed him, but at present he looked morose. Theodore, Gamadge's old colored servant, followed him muttering.

"All this noise and shoutin' around the house," said Theodore. "Can't hear yourself think. Why don't Harold fix the bells, now he's home? Can't get no repair men."

Harold said: "I can't fix the bells and the radio and the plumbing till I get the cat back into condition. And I can't work without tools. Somebody's been dusting my part of the laboratory. Can't find a thing."

"Harold says we've been rationing Martin," said Clara.

"He's the only member of the family that hasn't been," grumbled Theodore.

"Thin as a weasel," said Harold.

The yellow cat ran in and took up a commanding position on the hearth. Since Harold's return Martin had followed him everywhere. He did not like members of the family to disappear for long periods of time; Gamadge's theory was that he was trying to imagine the last twelve months an illusion, and to persuade himself that the permanence of things was unshaken.

"I wondered if you'd be willing to help me with a case," said Gamadge.

"Case?"

"I've just had sealed orders."

Harold took the buff envelope and its contents from Gamadge's hand, and sat down at the table to study them. Gamadge said: "Reason I called you, Clara: do you think your Aunt Rob knows the Fenways?"

"Mr. Blake Fenway and Caroline? She knows them, and I've met them. They aren't the case, are they?" Clara looked very much surprised.

"I don't know. Will you telephone and see if Miss Vauregard can come to lunch?"

Clara went to the telephone, and came back to say that her aunt would be with them in half an hour.

"Before she gets here I'll tell you and Harold the story."

They joined Harold at the round table in the window, the table that Theodore would soon be laying for lunch. Branches of a tall tree rose like a fretwork screen between the window and the backs of houses in the next street; snowflakes were beginning to fall from a lowering sky.

Gamadge finished the story of the paper balls. Harold looked alert, but Clara was non-plussed and incredulous.

"Henry," she said, "I think there must be some mistake. I really don't think you and Mr. Schenck can be right about this. There can't be anything terrible going on in the Fenway house."

"But I ought to find out, don't you think so? Even if the Fenways are untouchable, in the flattering sense, they're not forbidden to human speculation, are they?"

"No, but you sound as if you thought they were stuffy. They're not at all. The last time I met Mr. Fenway was at a wedding, and he's a perfect darling; and Caroline's very nice, too. She's rather sarcastic; or perhaps that isn't the right word."

"Embittered? Disillusioned?"

"Perhaps. But lots of fun to listen to."

"How old is she?"

"About thirty, I think."

"Good-looking?"

"Well, no; but very distinguished, and wears lovely clothes — plain but perfect."

Harold was studying the exhibits. He looked up at Gamadge. "The client must know a good deal about you," he said.

"Whatever the client knows, it seems to have inspired the client with more confidence than anybody except one person —" Gamadge smiled at his wife — "ever had in me before. I feel a horrid sense of responsibility, and the worst of it is that I'm a week late. If I don't hurry I may very well be too late, and hurry is impossible. And I'm taking on a job I really have no time for. I must make the most of this weekend." He looked at Harold. "Are you with me?"

"I'll start right in." Harold rose. "But I won't be able to work tonight. Mrs. Gamadge and I have a date."

"Date?" Gamadge looked suspiciously at his assistant, and from him to Clara.

"Dinner and theatre. Arline Prady is coming, and a friend of mine off a boat."

"I forbid it, I absolutely forbid it," said Gamadge violently.

"Henry!" protested Clara. "Harold's leave!"

"You'll get no cab, the buses will be jammed, it's starting to snow again, you'll catch your death. And this man off a boat — how horribly tough he will be!"

Harold was at the door. "Very nice feller," he said, "and wants to see the Planetarium."

22

2

UNTOUCHABLE

Clara's aunt, Miss Robina Vauregard, arrived in a hurry and said that she must dash away right after lunch. Gamadge allowed her to drink her cocktail and begin her lunch before he asked her to tell him all about the Fenways.

"Fenways? There's nothing to tell about the Fenways. Clara, the gutters are a foot under water, and the taxi man had to jump me across the curb." Miss Vauregard was always cheerful and chatty. "Now we're going to have more snow — in fact we are having it — and they say it's going to freeze again. How is your cold?"

"She got over it," said Gamadge. "She's going to get a new one tonight. Tell me about the Fenways, Miss Vauregard."

Her bright black eyes questioned him curiously. "Don't say they're in trouble! Nothing ever happens to *them!* At least —" she looked grave. "I shouldn't say that, but I was thinking of Blake and Mott and Caroline."

"Untouchables, are they?"

"The simplest, dearest creatures, and Blake is rather shy. I've always known them. Blake and Cort and I went to the same school here in New York when we were small; Mott was older, but I met him when I went to birthdays at Number 24. Old Mr. and Mrs. Fenway were always having parties for them. The school was Miss Denny's, and the little boys were in the basement. We played in the park afterwards. Them we went to other schools, but they came to our parties and we went to theirs, and we met at dancing school. I used to lead the German with one or the other of them often. Blake was quieter, but Cort was romantic."

"Just generally romantic?"

"Well, he was always in love with Belle Kane. He was nice to us all, but he was always in love with her. He finally married her, and she lives at Number 24 now. He died twenty years ago. Blake married such a lovely girl, just right for him. It's too bad Caroline looks like him, and not like her."

"Do you see much of them now?"

"Oh, no, I haven't for ages. We drifted apart, as people do unless they have something in common. I see Blake at people's houses sometimes, or at concerts or the theatre. Caroline is always with him now. She went to some college for a year or two — she's very in-

24

telligent, I believe — but after her mother died she came home. She and her father are devoted. It's such a shame — she had a most unfortunate experience with a man she was going to marry, but who married somebody else with more money."

"I thought the Fenways had money enough for anybody."

"She has none of her own yet. Blake and Cort were never great money-makers, you know; the money came from their grandfather, the one who sold all the original property. Blake's father was an only son, and inherited the whole property; he left it to Blake and Cort for life, and the capital to their children after they died. Caroline won't have her share until Blake dies."

"Mr. Cort Fenway had a son, I think; he's in possession of half the Fenway property now?"

Miss Vauregard's face clouded again. "Yes." After a moment she went on: "Blake's income must be pretty large, but he insists on keeping up those two great old houses — Number 24 and Fenbrook. This Fenbrook is only a little way up the Hudson, you know; the original Fenbrook was near Peekskill, a lovely place, built long before the Revolution. Poor Blake does regret it so; Grandfather Fenway sold it to the Van Broncks, neighbors of his, and they pulled down the house. There's a funny story about Blake which gives you a rather good idea of him, poor dear. Somebody once asked him about the old place, and he said it was torn down after the war. The person was surprised. 'As recently as that?' And Blake said in his innocent way: 'I mean the Revolutionary War.' "

Gamadge laughed, but said that Mr. Blake Fenway sounded agreeable.

"And he's not a fool, you know; just rather attached to the past."

"I'd like to meet him."

"That could be arranged, I should think, because he collects books. You might —" Miss Vauregard stopped, and fixed Gamadge with a lively and suspicious eye. "Henry, I will not turn you loose on the Fenways without knowing what you are up to."

"You think I'd be bad for them?" asked Gamadge, smiling.

"I don't think you could be, because they never get into trouble."

"Let's say that I know Mr. Fenway is interested in rare books. So am I. Won't that do?"

"I'm sure I heard that since he retired from practice he collects books. The family has always been interested in that kind of thing. Grandfather Fenway wrote, or something, and

I did hear that Caroline tried to."

"And was Mr. Cort Fenway literary too?"

"If he was, he couldn't have had much encouragement from Belle! We went to the same boarding school, and I can tell you that *she* wasn't literary! A most beautiful, brilliant girl, though, and so full of fun. But she had a most awful mother; excellent family, you know, but so vulgarly determined that Belle should make a rich match. *Anybody.* The awful woman used to fling Belle at the heads of the most impossible men. Belle wouldn't look at them, and we were all so glad when Cort Fenway got her at last. She was twenty-five by that time, and Mrs. Kane decided to relent. The other war was on — it was 1914. Cort was already there, a volunteer in France. He would be!"

"Like that, was he?"

"Oh, always. Belle and he were married in France, most romantic war wedding, and only came home in 1918 so that poor little Alden could be born here."

"Poor little Alden?"

Miss Vauregard paid no attention to the question, but rattled on: "Then Belle took him back to Europe when he was four, and she and Cort settled there; but Cort died in this country a year later. Belle was very comfortable over there; old Mr. Fenway was dead, and poor Alden had his share of the money. With guardians, of course; Blake Fenway is one of them. Belle would never have come back to America if it hadn't been for *this* awful war; and she was hurt getting on the awful boat they had to come home on."

"You keep saying 'poor' Alden."

"Such a tragedy! He was the loveliest baby, but when he was four they discovered that he would never develop mentally. Belle took him to all the foreign specialists, though, and she says they were wonderful; he's now as intelligent in some ways as a child of six or seven. She says that until you try to talk to him he seems quite normal, and that he's very handsome. Just a quiet, gentle creature, very well-behaved. You mustn't breathe a word of all this, Henry; hardly anybody knows it except the family and the doctors."

Gamadge was aware that Clara was looking at him with a certain anxiety. He asked: "Have you seen him?"

"No, but I've seen Belle. I called at Number 24 in the autumn of 1940, when I heard that she was at home. I'm ashamed to say that I haven't been back again, but you know what it's like in New York, and now there's all the war work. I'm on at least four committees, and I never do anything else. Blake Fenway was an angel to them, Belle said; wouldn't hear of her taking Alden to a hotel. Of course she can't run a house or an apartment while she's tied to a wheel chair, and she wouldn't dream of putting Alden in an institution, even the best private one. She's never been parted from him since he was born."

"How badly hurt is she? Can she get about on crutches?"

"Not yet; the injury was partly to her back, and some nerves were involved. But she's much better; she's had regular surgical treatment and massage, and of course their old family doctor, Thurley, takes the best care of her. He brought Alden into the world. He says she'll be walking in another year or less; he told me so himself when I met him at the movies only a month ago."

"The boy has an attendant of some kind, I suppose?"

"Belle was very lucky about that. While they were trying to get to Marseilles — such an awful experience — ghastly — an old school friend of ours turned up; when I knew her she was Alice Horton. She's a widow now, Alice Grove. She had a young niece in tow, or rather her husband's niece, who'd been at school in Switzerland. Alice's money was all tied up in Paris, so Belle instantly took her on as courier and companion. Most fortunately; because Belle was injured before they ever left the dock at Marseilles. Alice Grove took care of her on the voyage, and takes care of her now; she doesn't need a nurse any more."

"What became of the niece?"

"She's at Number 24 too, doing some kind of secretarial work for Blake Fenway; or didn't they say that she was very outdoor, and spends her time up at Fenbrook? Well; who should turn up on the dock but a young fellow named Craddock, whom Alice knew. His parents were old friends of her husband's. He was a newspaperman in China, and he was going home because he'd acquired some obscure kind of germ, and had intermittent fever. He was the perfect companion for Alden, Belle says he's wonderful with him. She dreads the time when he'll be well enough to be drafted."

"And *he's* at Number 24?"

"Oh, yes; a fixture."

"And this Mr. Mott Fenway —"

"He's always been there, or at Fenbrook. He failed in business when he was a young man, and he's lived with his cousin Blake ever since. I believe he does estate work and accounts for him."

"The household consists, then, of Mr. Blake Fenway, from whom all blessings flow; his daughter Caroline, whom Clara thinks sarcastic, and who may have some reason for being so; Mr. Mott Fenway, an elderly dependent;

Mrs. Cort Fenway, crippled and tied to an invalid chair; her son, a mental invalid; his attendant, a semi-invalid with recurrent fever; her companion and the companion's niece, indigent."

"You sound so grim, Henry!"

"It can't be a jolly house, now can it?"

"But the Fenways never think of Mott as a poor relation, they love having him there; and the Fenway sense of family obligation is very great — of course they'd have Belle and Alden. They're as well off as Blake, you know; probably better off than he is, because they haven't his expenses. And Alden is no trouble; I told you he'd had all those specialists — Viborg here, until he was four, and then *everybody* in Europe. Belle said he had the best men in Austria, and Fagon in Paris. She was with him at the most wonderful sanatoria. And then this fearful war came, and it set him back. The travelling and the hardships were bad for him. He's more silent now."

"Still, he's a liability in a household."

"Belle insists not. And young Craddock is getting well. And the Groves earn their salaries, I suppose."

"Is there any record of mental disease in the Fenway family — or on the Kane side of the connection?"

"Not that I ever heard of. The only neurotic

I ever knew about was Mrs. Kane, and with her it was only hysterics and bad temper."

"Why on earth didn't she allow her daughter to marry Cort Fenway in the beginning?"

"He wasn't a catch then. Mrs. Kane wouldn't care anything about family or distinction, she only wanted money to be kept in luxury on. Cort didn't have much until his father died."

"Did the old gentleman know that Alden Fenway was mentally deficient when he left him the capital of half his property?"

"Good Heavens, no! He died when the poor child was only two. I don't think he and old Mrs. Fenway approved of that match, you know; they detested Mrs. Kane. But they had a horror of family dissension, and they were so fond of Cort, and Belle was supposed to have settled down; then Mrs. Kane died, and Cort was given a nice income. It's so sad — he didn't live to enjoy it more than two or three years."

"And the name of Fenway dies with the unfortunate Alden. How about old Mrs. Fenway, Cort's mother? When did she depart?"

"Just before old Mr. Fenway did."

Gamadge passed cigarettes to Miss Vauregard, took one himself, and lighted hers and his own. He asked: "Did you see this Mrs. Grove when you called on Mrs. Cort Fenway two years ago?"

"Yes. It's extraordinary how little changed she is since boarding school. She must be fifty-five at least, she was a year or so older than Belle; but she's the same quiet, determined little thing, only drier and cooler. She had a lot of moral influence, you know, and a will of iron. I thought Belle seemed very meek with her even now; she was laying down the law to poor Belle about their fancywork. They're doing an immense job of needle point for the drawing-room furniture."

"You didn't see young Craddock or the Grove girl?"

"No, he was out walking with Alden, and I think the girl was up at Fenbrook. She was going over the books up there for Blake, and Belle said some of them were turning out to be quite valuable. They had book catalogues on the table; quite keen they were."

"I ought to get on with the whole family — when you've given me that letter of introduction to Mr. Blake Fenway."

"Henry, if I'm to introduce you, I must know why!"

"It's part of an enquiry on behalf of a client who wishes to remain anonymous."

"Please do it, Aunt Robbie," begged Clara.

"You know Henry wouldn't ask you unless it was very important."

"Well, I suppose I can oblige with a clear conscience; there can't be anything wrong at Number 24."

Clara's chow stepped into the room. He paused to convince himself that there was no feline presence on the hearth, and then walked over and lay down in front of the fire.

Gamadge said, smiling at Miss Vauregard: "We have two tawny animals in the house. They belong to races that don't as a rule get on, but they get on very well; if they didn't, one of them would have to go, and they know it as well as Clara and I do."

"Yes, but Henry, these *are* animals!" When he said nothing, but continued to smoke and to look at her smilingly, she waved her hands, expressing surrender. "Very well, but you'll have to tell me what to say."

"I'd like to call you up after I've seen a bookseller named Hall. Blake Fenway has dealings with him, and he may give us a lead." Gamadge rose. "It's Saturday, but I don't think he'll have left his office; he practically lives there. I'll call him."

The telephone conversation took only a couple of minutes. When he came back, Gamadge said: "He'll be in the office. When I've seen him I'll call you. Do you think you could send the note around to Mr. Fenway afterwards by hand?"

"Of course; but you seem to be in a dreadful hurry."

"I am; and I'm more grateful to you than I can ever —"

Miss Vauregard would not listen. "It's nothing, nothing at all. Good gracious Heavens, can it be three o'clock?"

"We didn't finish our cocktails," said Clara, "till after two."

"So we didn't. I must run."

Half an hour later Harold strolled into the library.

"I hung around Number 24 from two-thirty on," he said, "but nobody threw anything out of a window."

"The postman doesn't call on Saturday afternoon. Of course there was no paper ball."

"The old man came around at three-fifteen and went over the premises with a microscope; picked up everything in sight, and dusted snow off the steps and sidewalk. Snow kept on coming down, so he finally gave it up. The paper ball didn't come out of any of the basement windows, they're icebound; those on the front, I mean. The ones on the avenue are clear, and one was partly open; kitchen, I suppose. I don't think the paper was thrown from the top story, it wouldn't have cleared the roof

35

of the bay window without falling outside the railings. It came from the middle bay window on the second or third floor."

Clara said: "Alden Fenway didn't throw it out; nobody with a six- or seven-year-old brain made up that message."

"Somebody might get him to throw it out for them," suggested Harold. Then he stared at her. "Do you mean he's a child of six or seven?"

"He's twenty-five; mentally retarded," said Gamadge. Harold asked, after a pause: "Could he be trusted to throw a message out of a window without letting anybody see him do it?"

"Could be, perhaps; I don't know. Wouldn't be, if discovery of the message meant serious consequences to the sender."

Harold frowned. "We don't know how crazy he is. He may not be as crazy as they think. Suppose Mr. Schenck is right, and he has lucid spells, and is trying to get some information to you while the spell lasts?"

"Alden Fenway was pronounced mentally incurable when he was four years old, by a great authority on brain disease. His mind developed a little, but it could never develop into a mature mind. He wouldn't have lucid spells; he'd always be on the same low level of intelligence, if he didn't eventually sink lower."

"What do you think of this, then? At three-five a young fellow came down the left-hand steps — it's a double flight — and hailed a cab; big light-haired feller, quite handsome, stoops a little. Just as the cab came along to the curb he crumpled up a piece of paper and threw it away."

Clara's voice was almost a shriek: "Threw away a piece of paper?"

Harold continued stolidly: "White paper. Then he turned and looked around at another young feller who came out of the house and ran down the steps. Thin guy, pale, black hair, homely face, old belted mackintosh. This feller picked up the paper, looked at it, and went to the corner rubbish basket and chucked it in. Then he came back and took the big feller by the arm; helped him into the cab."

"Harold," gasped Clara, "didn't you get that piece of paper out of that rubbish basket?"

Harold produced a crushed scrap. "Here it is."

Clara seized and unfolded it. "Well," she said, "we know one thing; Alden Fenway can play tit-tat-toe."

Gamadge looked at the untidy squares and the noughts and crosses. He said: "Perhaps he had help, perhaps he always gets beaten. But if those two young men were Alden Fenway and the Mr. Craddock who looks after him, we know something else — neither of them is my client; they both have too much liberty to be forced into throwing messages out of a window."

Harold said: "Young Fenway hasn't much liberty; Craddock was after him like lightning."

"But he got out of the house alone, and he had time to slip a note to the cabdriver; hadn't he?"

"Yes, I suppose he had. He's a big, good-looking feller; I thought he must be lame or sick; I wouldn't have known there was anything the matter with his brain. But of course I didn't know there was a mental case in the house, and it's no use now to say that I thought he didn't have any more expression than the face of a clock. Lots of people don't, anyway."

"I'll take your word for his expression. Any more happenings?"

"As soon as the cab drove off, a nice car came along. Oldish man got out, nice-looking, carried a bag; looked like a doctor. He went in the house. Then the old guy arrived, and started in with his broom, and I came away."

"Very nice scouting. Bring your friend and Arline here for cocktails this evening."

Harold's dark face was illumined by a slow

smile. He said: "O.K. Like you to meet Corporal Lipowitsky. Quite a dancer."

Clara said: "I can't wait. What an evening."

3

GAMADGE BUYS A BOOK

Gamadge went out into a thin, icy snowfall, and along streets piled high at the curbs with Thursday's snow. He crossed a deserted avenue, waited long for a bus, and when it came waded to it. Dismounting in the lower forties, he ploughed westward with his collar up, his hatbrim down, and his hands sunk in his pockets.

He went into a converted brownstone house where J. Hall occupied the second floor. J. Hall's show window was bare but impressive, with its reticent display of open folios, a map, a set of faded small octavos in red morocco gilt, and a framed copperplate engraving, dusky and mellow. Gamadge climbed dark stairs and opened a half-glass door, on which gold letters said merely: *J. Hall. Books.*

He entered a large front room which had once been somebody's parlor; books rose to its moulded cornices. Hall's desk stood beside the window, Hall's clerk's desk had its modest place in a corner, beside folding doors. These led to the back office, where Hall informally received a chosen few.

Hall's clerk was at his desk, reading under a green-shaded light. He was a serious young man, whose very hair looked dusty. He rose. "Mr. Hall's expecting you, Mr. Gamadge."

"Thanks, Albert."

"It's an awful day."

"It's an awful day."

Albert opened a folding door. Gamadge paused beside his desk. "What are you reading? *Men Working*?"

"Yes, sir. Business is a little slow."

"You don't say."

Gamadge went through the doorway into a sanctum warmed by a coal fire. J. Hall sat hunched over this, whiskey at his elbow, his face obscured by the large silk handkerchief on which he was blowing his nose. By birth an Englishman, he had been an American citizen for nearly forty years; but he adhered as faithfully as he could to the customs of his native land. Before he went home Albert would bring him a pot of tea.

He looked at Gamadge over his shoulder, and put the bandanna away. "I have a frightful cold," he said. "Have some medicine?"

"No, thanks." Gamadge sat down at the other end of the hearth.

"I'd retire, if I could find a cheap, sunny

place with no arty people and no trippers. Did you come to buy something? The Cotter collection? Diaries, portraits — mostly proof impressions — and private plates of great rarity. Fine and scarce mezzotints. The whole bound up in half green levant by Rivière."

"I read about it in your circular. Don't try me on it; try customers like — er — Mr. Blake Fenway."

This produced a choleric stare from Hall. "Fenway? A lot you seem to know about Fenway. He doesn't buy that kind of thing, or much of anything. Not now. But he's fond of books in his simple way, and I like to oblige him; he's a gentleman."

"What's his contemptible hobby?"

"Latish American first, too late for big values. He likes to fill out the authors that his parents and grandparents bought as current literature; nice idea. The Fenway books are in mint condition — dare say they weren't read. But they were bought — Howells back to Hawthorne." J. Hall got out his handkerchief again, sneezed into it, and went on: "We were in a quandary about Henry James, because the Fenways only possessed *Daisy Miller*. But we think we'll fill him out when the war's over."

"That will be quite a job."

"Quite. Fenway has stopped buying books

until then, and who am I to protest? He'd trade, but he has nothing I want — naturally."

"Naturally."

"I have the *Elsie Venner* he wanted; his is the wrong one, the one that has no misprint in it. He was dreadfully dashed when he found that out. Dreadfully dashed."

Gamadge said: "I might take yours off your hands if you don't stick me too much for it."

"Good God! Albert — a sale."

The dusty Albert appeared, smiling.

"Wrap up the *Elsie Venner* for Mr. Gamadge. We have no boys, Gamadge; will Albert have to drag it uptown for you, or will you take it yourself?"

"Since you put it like that, I'll take it myself."

"I don't mind delivering it, Mr. Gamadge." Albert had climbed up on a stepladder, and was removing two faded brown volumes from a shelf.

"I don't mind taking it. I'm going home in a cab — I'm not dressed for Alpine climbing. Is that novel in there for sale, Albert? The one you're reading?"

J. Hall stared. "Novel? Current novel? Why don't you go to your corner rental library?"

"I want to buy it."

Albert had retired to his desk, and was wrapping the parcel. He desisted, to say: "You can have it, Mr. Gamadge. I can get myself another on my way home."

"Mighty good of you." Gamadge handed Albert the retail price and tax, and Albert included *Men Working* in the package. "By the way." Gamadge pulled on his gloves. "Did you jot my name down in pencil on one of the office envelopes, Albert, and then mail it by mistake?"

"If he did," said J. Hall from his armchair, "I'll fire him. We waste no stationery nowadays."

Albert, looking mystified, had shaken his head. "No, sir. I never jotted your name down anywhere."

Gamadge jerked his head towards the back room, and soundlessly inquired: "Did *he?*"

Albert shook his head again. "No, sir."

"What's all this?" J. Hall craned to look at Gamadge. "Did you get such a thing?"

"Yes. Minor mystery; if I solve it I'll try to remember to tell you about it."

"You might solve Fenway's mystery for him."

"Fenway's?" Gamadge, his parcel under his arm, went and looked at the back of J. Hall's head. "What mystery?"

"He's lost a plate out of an old book of views. Wants another, but I think it's unprocurable. That collection is in private hands

44

or museums of Americana. Not much value."

"What was the plate?"

"Colored plate of the old place they had up the Hudson — Fenbrook. I'll advertise, but I don't think he'll get one."

"When did he discover the loss?"

"Last week. Telephoned me about it on Monday."

"What happened to his rule about not buying until after the war?"

"Oh, the rule doesn't apply to his book of views. That's a family matter; he'd pay anything to get his picture back."

Gamadge took his departure. As soon as he reached home he put the parcel of books away in his office, and then called Miss Vauregard.

"I have the information we need," he said.

"Then won't you just dictate a letter, Henry? I'll get a pencil."

When she returned to the telephone he had prepared a couple of notes. He said: "You'll probably want to put in something about being sorry you never see them any more — just to break the ice."

"I should think so!"

"And you'll want to ask how Mrs. Cort Fenway is getting along, that kind of thing. Then you might say: 'My niece's husband, Henry Gamadge, has been hearing about your American first editions from Jervis Hall, the bookseller, and he's dying to see them. I think he buys books himself from Mr. Hall sometimes, in a modest way. If you'd care to call him up, I know he'd be much gratified. The trouble is, it would have to be rather soon, because he's going away again on some war work.' "

"Oh, Henry," wailed Miss Vauregard, "are you?"

"Well, not immediately; that's just to hurry him up a little. Then you might put in something about being quite fond of me, and what a nice intelligent fellow I am. But for Heaven's sake don't say anything about crime."

"Crime? Oh — your cases."

"Mightn't they scare him?"

"Well — if he's heard about them he'll still be willing to meet you, for my sake; but he may not let you meet the family!"

"I must try to make a good impression on him. And I can't tell you how I appreciate this. Can't begin to."

"It's all right, dear."

"You'll send it around by hand?"

"He'll have it in an hour." She paused. "Henry — you're not getting some kind of occupational disease, I hope?"

"What kind?"

"Thinking things are wrong when nothing *is* wrong?"

"Perhaps I am. I'll go carefully."

As the cocktail hour approached, Harold came into the library to find Gamadge sitting on the chesterfield in front of the fire, his cigarette going out between his fingers and his eyes fixed on vacancy. Harold asked: "Find out anything from Hall?"

"My message didn't originate in his office. Fenway isn't my client — he telephoned to Hall on Monday."

"Somebody standing over him with a gun, perhaps."

"They wouldn't risk it. He might get something to Hall in code. Lots of chances when you're talking old books, as my message proves."

"I don't think he can be the client."

The telephone rang. Harold went into the hall and brought the instrument back on its long cord. He said: "Mr. Blake Fenway to speak to Mr. Gamadge."

Gamadge said: "Mr. Fenway? This is Henry Gamadge speaking."

A pleasant voice replied: "I'm very glad to find you at home, Mr. Gamadge. I've just come in myself, and found a note from our dear Robina Vauregard. If you're really interested in my books I shall be delighted to show them to you."

Gamadge said: "Thank you very much indeed. Miss Vauregard was here to lunch with us. She said she'd write."

"I have *your* charming books, and I shall be greatly honored to meet the writer. I hope Hall warned you that I'm a mere amateur at book collecting."

"We're all mere amateurs to J. Hall."

Fenway laughed. "You should see him looking for Melville and Poe among my Aldriches and Stocktons!"

"The only trouble is, Mr. Fenway, that I really have only a very few days —"

"So I understand. Could you make time tomorrow, and drop in after lunch for coffee? I'm sorry to say that I have a lunch engagement; our local citizen's committee meets when it can."

"Half past two?"

"Splendid. I'm sorry that I shan't have all the family books to show you; a good many of them are still up at Fenbrook. I'm having the more valuable things sent down by degrees. I never realized until now, when I have a certain amount of leisure, that Fenbrook isn't the safest place for books in case of fire."

"These are not times to risk losing anything that's old."

"No, are they? Tomorrow, then."

"Thank you very much."

Gamadge returned the telephone to Sergeant Bantz. He said: "Mr. Blake Fenway is not my client. He goes where he likes."

"I heard that part of it. Nice-sounding feller."

"I should judge him the kindest, most considerate and least harmful of created beings."

"Which makes it all a little crazier. What's going on in his house?"

The first of the cocktail guests entered the library; Miss Arline Prady, a tall, plain, bony girl with large dark eyes. She was a ballet dancer out of a job, at present engaged in filling out programmes for camp entertainments. She liked to wear the latest thing, if that thing happened to be inexpensive and conspicuous, and this evening she wore a knitted woolen head-shawl or fascinator of the brightest purple, a short, woolly coat, a red dress, and high boots. The slightly leftist effect of the costume was far from Miss Prady's intention, for she had no politics.

Corporal Lipowitsky was not far behind her, and Clara hurried in a minute later, dressed in her best for the corporal. Gamadge exerted himself for the party, which (but for Clara) looked as if it were going to be a solemn one. Gamadge rather wished he knew what the dinner conversation was going to be like. He poured cocktails, passed canapés, and tried to introduce a note of frivolity into the proceedings. At last he adjusted snow boots to Clara's feet, and saw the revellers off.

He retuned to eat his own dinner. *Was* he getting an occupation disease, he wondered? This case, if it was a case, oppressed and frightened him. He couldn't settle down to other work, and after he had had his coffee he dragged on his outdoor things again and went doggedly into the dark streets. He walked uptown, approaching the Fenway house from the rear.

It reminded him of those pleasant old chromos that used to hang in pairs on cottage walls — *Life In The City, Life In The Country*. Here was *Life In The City,* it's very tone and quality restored by the dim-out and the storm. The big, square brick house in its snowy grounds looked cosy and festive; yellow light from its windows filtered out on the whiteness of the garden, and on its bushes and leafless trees. One was a sycamore; each of the brown balls that adhered to its upper branches had a little cap of snow.

He went on to the corner. A taxi — it would no doubt have been a fine town car some days earlier, but the pleasure-driving ban was in force — drove up to the curb opposite the double flight of steps. Two silk-hatted men stepped out, and one lady. She was furred to the ears in sable, with multicolored earrings just showing above her collar. She had dark hair, and a plain, dark, aquiline face.

"Be careful, Miss Fenway," said one of the men, and the other raised an umbrella. Strange, hard times for these people.

The front door closed behind them. Gamadge lighted a cigarette and turned to walk home. A double shadow moved in front of him, the paler half of which did not seem to have any connection with the other or with himself. Like this phantom of a case, he thought; a dim, doubtful, formless thing that couldn't be accounted for unless one had special knowledge.

He went home and did some work. Clara and Sergeant Bantz came in, not very late; Harold looked gratified.

"Lipowitsky had a fine time," he said. "Told me so. He thinks New York girls are fine."

Gamadge, with a glance at his wife, said he was glad Lipowitsky wasn't disappointed.

"I suppose nothing more turned up about the case?" Harold asked it idly.

"Oh — one thing more. My client isn't Miss Caroline Fenway."

4

THE BOOK OF VIEWS

At half past two o'clock on Sunday, January 31st, Gamadge stood in bright sunshine, a book under his arm, and took a corner view of the Fenway house. Even in daylight it had a semiurban look; he could imagine ladies with parasols walking in the garden on fine afternoons, and old Mr. Fenway driving down to business every morning in a barouche.

He strolled down the side street, past the double flight of stone steps. There was the bay window; there, below and in front of it, the spot where the paper balls had lain. Beyond stretched the high brick wall with the dark-green door in it. He mounted the nearer flight and looked into a neatly paved side yard, with shrubs and a row of trees against the wall that divided the Fenway grounds from the next house.

He rang, and entered a Pompeian vestibule with painted walls and ceiling. Black-and-white marble was underfoot, and facing him were ponderous walnut doors, their upper

52

halves of glass frosted in pseudoclassic designs. The Fenways certainly had the sense of the past. A very old manservant admitted him, said that Mr. Fenway expected him, and took away his hat and coat; he retained his book, however, carrying it with what he hoped was an absent-minded air as he followed the old butler down the hall.

He had a glimpse into immense reaches of drawing room on the left, of a bay-windowed dining room on the right. A broad stairway rose into dimness; at the turn of the second-floor landing he saw a niche, with Psyche (marble) holding a lamp. Oil lamp; they couldn't very well wire Psyche.

At the end of the hall a glassed door let in a filtered, grayish light; by it could be distinguished a door under the stairs (coat cupboard?) another beyond (back drawing room?) and two opposite. The butler opened the last of these.

"Mr. Gamadge."

Gamadge entered a fine big library, panelled and ceiled in oak, with two windows looking out on the lawn, and a bay window overlooking the side garden. A slender man came forward; clean-shaven, gray-haired, with a long, well-shaped head and kind blue eyes. The aquiline features that made his daughter a plain woman made Blake Fenway a handsome man;

he was excellently dressed in the darkest town clothes.

"This is a very great pleasure, Mr. Gamadge." He shook hands with Gamadge, who replied that he was aware *he* owed it to Miss Vauregard.

"Not at all, I am delighted to have the opportunity of meeting you. Your books — really extraordinary. Literary detection. Absorbing."

"Great fun to do." Gamadge glanced about him; at the high bookshelves with their cupboards and their glass doors, surmounted by busts of classical lawgivers and writers; at solid furniture, red-velvet curtains and upholstery, impressive bric-a-brac, a thick old Turkey rug. There was a portrait above the mantel, with Blake Fenway's features but a thinner and less agreeable mouth.

There was a coffee table in front of the fire. The butler came in from a door in the north wall, carrying a tray and an after-dinner coffee service. He set it down.

"Thank you, Phillips, and you needn't wait," said Fenway. "Mr. Gamadge, will you have that chair?"

Gamadge sat down in the chair opposite Fenway's, and accepted a cigar. Phillips went away; Fenway poured coffee. When Gamadge had his cup, Fenway glanced — not for the first time — at the book which Gamadge had laid on the little table beside him.

"Have you brought something to show me?" he asked. "I hope so."

"It's just something I borrowed — to read."

"I'm afraid I don't keep up with the current authors as I should. My daughter warns me that that's a sign of advancing years, and that I ought to fight the tendency." He smiled. "She says fiction gives one the contemporary background. Well, Caroline is always right; but when I read fiction, I want fiction, you know; I don't want a document!"

"There's a lot to be said for your point of view. But even your favorites —" Gamadge's eye wandered along the shelves nearest him — "even they don't quite keep their social bias out of their novels."

"Perhaps," laughed Fenway, "mine is the same as theirs!"

"Let's see them."

They walked from section to section of the cases, stopping to glance at the books Mr. Fenway pulled out, discussing certain finds and special treasures. At last, when they had reached the end of the east wall, Gamadge said: "There's your *Elsie Venner,* I see. All correct, I suppose, misprint and all."

Mr. Fenway looked mortified. "I'm ashamed to say it isn't. I had no idea ours wasn't the real, right thing until Hall enlightened me. It really makes me very restless not to *have* the right one; with everything else right, you know. But I don't feel justified in indulging a hobby these days, with such a crying want of money for the war needs."

Gamadge said: "I have the real right one."

"You have!" Mr. Fenway gazed at him with baffled longing.

"And I don't in the least want it. Look here, Mr. Fenway; why shouldn't we do a trade?"

"A trade? What can I possibly have that you do want?"

"Well, you have a duplicate *William Henry Letters*. Mine was read to pulp when I was a boy. If you cared to part with one of them, and with your *Elsie Venner* —"

"You don't mean it? The deal wouldn't be at all a fair one."

"I can consult J. Hall. There won't be much cash difference."

"My dear Mr. Gamadge, you really have no idea what a favor you're doing me."

"None at all, but I know how you feel. I used to buy firsts myself."

"I'll have the books sent down to your house today, and the man can pick up your Holmes."

"Not at all; I'll take them with me in a cab, and bring your book along tonight or tomorrow."

"What fun it all is — these discoveries and coincidences! And what a piece of luck for me! I must tell Caroline about it, and my sister-in-law and her friend Mrs. Grove will be much interested too. They're looking forward to meeting, you in any case. When we've finished here we'll go up."

Gamadge was a little amused and much gratified to find that he had passed his examinations; but there was a final one to come. It came while Fenway closed the glass door of the last bookshelf:

"I believe you do your duty as a citizen in a way that few of us are qualified to do it," he said. "Our firm has never practised in the criminal branch of the law, but we have always had the highest respect for those who face the more disagreeable aspects of it — and for criminologists in general."

Gamadge, laughing, said that he never hoped to hear a handsomer tribute to detective investigation. He added: "I'm afraid the puzzle element in it is the element that attracts me. I can't profess to be actuated by loftier motives when I take a case."

Mr. Fenway seemed delighted. "A hobby; I thought so!"

"But not," said Gamadge, "exactly a sport."

"No, no; it could never be that. You don't —" Mr. Fenway hesitated, and then went on in an apologetic tone — "you don't do this work professionally?"

Gamadge laughed again. "I've been retained, some times, but now I come to think of it I've never been paid yet!"

Mr. Fenway was more pleased than ever, but he grew grave. "I always like to find that we are not entirely commercial now, but you put me in something of a quandary. I have a little problem of my own which I should be very glad to consult you about, but if I consulted another lawyer, or a doctor, I should expect to reimburse him for giving me the benefit of his experience."

"I have no professional standing, Mr. Fenway; and as I said, I like little problems." Gamadge hoped that he did not sound eager. "Let me hear what yours is. But if it's about books, you know, I'm no expert; J. Hall's your man."

Fenway said: "Hall has no opinion on the matter, and I don't suppose even you will have one. However." He turned to a long table in the embrasure of the west window. It was heaped with what looked like an odd lot of books, some not entirely out of their wrappings; two slender dark-green quartos lay among them. He lifted first one and then the other. "Now what," he murmured, "can Caroline have done with Volume III?"

"Can I help, sir?"

"No, no. This is the last lot that little Hilda Grove sent down from Fenbrook. Such a good child. Now where on earth. . . . Wait! I remember."

He crossed the room to a buhl table at the right of the hall door; its surface was almost hidden by a large, flat-topped coffer of metal thickly inlaid with ivory; Fenway raised the lid.

"Here it is," he said, and withdrew another of the dark-green books, which Gamadge now saw to be bound in velvet.

"If you'll just sit down again, Mr. Gamadge, and look at this?"

Gamadge resumed his seat beside the fire, and took the quarto on his knees. It was lettered in gold: *Views On The Hudson.*

Fenway sat down opposite him; he watched him open it, glance at the charmingly colored frontispiece, and then look at the title page.

Views On The Hudson, he read, *With Descriptions by Several Hands. In Four Volumes. Coloured Plates by Pidgeon. 1835.* He turned leaves. "What a nice set."

Fenway looked sad. "It *was* a nice set, Mr. Gamadge. If you'll turn to page 50 . . ."

On page 50 Gamadge read: "Description of Fenbrook, the old Fenway residence near Peekskill. By Julian Fenway, Esq." He lifted his eyes to his host. "Was that your grand-father, sir?"

"That was my grandfather."

"But there seems to be no picture of Fenbrook here."

"No; as you see, it has been torn out."

Gamadge discerned a trace of ragged edge where the plate had been, and another trace of its protective tissue. He said: "This is shocking!"

"You can imagine how I felt, when I looked for the picture and found that it was gone. But perhaps you can't, unless you happen to know that the original house was torn down in 1849, and that that view was all we had left of old Fenbrook. The set is irreplaceable; some of the landowners combined and had the books made and the views taken; there is none, Hall thinks, on the market. Fenbrook was a plain little house, and my grandfather doesn't seem to have cared much about it; he let a friend have it and the rest of that property; my father never saw it."

Gamadge expressed his sympathy by a groan.

"The poor old gentleman," continued Fenway, "my grandfather, of course I mean, didn't do badly in the financial sense by the deal; he bought property here and in West-chester county, and in the 60's he built himself this house and the new Fenbrook; they were, I can assure you, the latest thing. You should have seen the delightful house downtown that my father was born in! That went, too. So now we have this, which even to me, with all my sentiment for it, isn't a model of architectural beauty; and one of the same period up the Hudson, completely suburban of course, and (I can assure you) well bracketed!"

"I'm sure it has immense dignity and charm."

"Nobody but a Fenway would live in it. At least I have one thing to be thankful for — my poor brother Cort never knew that the picture of old Fenbrook would be lost. He was very fond of these books. I can see him now, sitting in the library up there with Volume III on his knees. We had a project even then, and I looked forward to carrying it out — until now. There's not much point in it now. I wanted to write a little history of our family here — we're extinct in England — for the Historical Society. Of course the view of Fenbrook and Grandfather's description of it would have been the most important — the only important part of the thing. That's why I had the books sent down; I've retired from law practice, and I thought it would be a delightful way of spending my leisure."

"It's tough, Mr. Fenway."

"Well, now, Mr. Gamadge," and Fenway, sitting back in his chair, looked at his guest with a smile, "you're to tell me what can have become of the view of Fenbrook."

"Am I?" Gamadge returned the smile.

"That's my little problem. Mind you, I don't hope to get it back, because it may have vanished at any time in the last twenty years; I haven't looked for it since my brother died. But I should like a mind trained in these mysteries to tell me why on earth it and only it should have been torn out of the book, and what can have been done with it."

Gamadge became grave. "I shouldn't in the least mind discussing the possibilities, but it wouldn't be an intelligent discussion unless we included all of them."

"Of course, all of them." Fenway looked surprised. "Why not?"

"My type of mind is a very aggravating one, you know; it pursues a question long after more comfortable minds are ready and willing to drop it. I may bore you."

"Bore me? I venture to say that you are incapable of doing that, Mr. Gamadge."

"Well, to make a beginning." Gamadge looked down at the open book on his knees. "You saw the picture twenty years ago?"

"A little less than that. My brother was up at Fenbrook shortly before he died — very suddenly, of pneumonia — in the summer of 1923."

"Where were the books kept?"

"In cases very much like these, in the Fenbrook library."

"Not locked up?"

"No, we had nothing we thought valuable there; I mean to thieves."

"When did they reach you here in New York?"

"They arrived on Thursday afternoon, the twenty-first. I opened the parcel there on that table, but I had no time to look at them until Friday evening, after dinner."

"This young lady — Miss Grove — sent them down?"

"By express, with some others, on Tuesday. We don't of course use the station wagon now for such work. It only goes out for necessary shopping. Hilda, of course, was distressed when I called her up about the view; I had a first faint hope that it might have loosened, and that it would be found somewhere in the library. But it was torn out, that's obvious."

"Miss Grove has looked for it?"

"She's looked everywhere. We don't go up there ourselves except in warm weather; we're conserving coal. The Dobsons — a very nice couple who have been with us a long time — keep part of the house warm for themselves and Hilda. It must be lonely for her." Fenway's expression was doubtful. "But she insists not; she won't complain. She's a niece — or niece by marriage, rather — of my sister-in-law's friend and companion, Mrs. Grove; did I mention her before? My sister-in-law was badly injured on her trip here from France in 1940 — a most terrible experience it all was. She is still unable to walk, but otherwise she's greatly improved. Mrs. Grove takes care of her; an admirable arrangement."

"I should think it would be, if Mrs. Grove is an old friend."

"Actually a school friend."

Gamadge was again studying the place where the view of Fenbrook had been. He said: "The plate and the tissue guard were both removed; but of course if the plate were torn out the tissue guard would go with it. We may forget the disappearance of the guard. Our question is, why was the plate torn out? Well, there are certain more or less familiar reasons for removing illustrations from books; we might consider them first. There is the nefarious process known as grangerizing, more politely known as enlarging."

"I don't think I ever heard of it."

"Since late in the eighteenth century it's been a hobby with certain persons who have plenty of leisure, like to handle books, and enjoy light manual labor. They feel they're creating something, and of course a granger-ized set is unique; at the expense of many other books, out of which the illustrations have been ripped incontinent."

"But who could possibly want a view of old Fenbrook for any such purpose as that?"

"I can't imagine, unless somebody else was inspired to write up the Fenway family."

"I have my share of family conceit, I suppose," said Fenway, smiling, "but even I don't think there's any such person. There are no Fenways left but myself, my daughter, and my cousin Mott. And my nephew. They are all out of the question."

"And we may assume that the Historical Society isn't collecting for its archives — er — informally. Well, to proceed: people have been known to take pictures out of books in order to frame them and hang them on the wall, or to paste them on lamp shades and waste-baskets. I see on the lamp shade beside you, for instance, a rather charming woodcut portrait of —" Gamadge leaned forward — "of Theophrastus. If it wasn't once in a book, I'll eat it and the lamp shade too."

Fenway started, looked guilty, and glanced sidelong at the portrait of Theophrastus. He said: "Caroline got the lamp shade for me at a decorator's. I assure you that nothing of the sort has been done with the view of Fenbrook."

"Can you be sure? I'm sorry to say that I once found, among my grandmother's effects, a topographical view of old Albany behind a photograph — with whiskers — of my grandfather."

"It's inconceivable that anyone connected with this family should have done anything of the kind."

"Unlikely, I agree with you; and easy to disprove by a glance at the backs of the Fenbrook pictures. The superposing process wouldn't be a professional job. Grandfather Gamadge was clamped into place with two carpet tacks and a piece of mending tape. Well, now I'm going to shock you again. Children are known to tear or deface the pages of books; spill things on them. I say children, because older persons would confess the damage; but a young child might tear that page out; thereby not only protecting itself, but (according to child logic) making the damage nonexistent."

Fenway did look shocked; he also looked uneasy. "The books were behind glass; no strange children had access to them, certainly no visiting small fry. And of course Caroline was incapable of treating a book in that way; like all of us, she took good care of her books.

And if by some accident she had spoiled the picture, I can only assure you that she would have told me about it. She was not brought up," and he raised his eyes to the portrait above the mantel, "quite as strictly as my generation was, you know; she had no fear of me. At the time — when I last saw the view, you know — she must have been eleven years old. Far too old . . . Oh, impossible."

"Your nephew?"

"Alden wasn't here; he was with his mother in Europe."

"Who dusted the books in those days, and who does it now?"

"Responsible persons then as now, who wouldn't dislodge a picture by accident, much less deface it and tear it out. I think the books are only dusted at long intervals; they're in presumably dust proof cases."

"Who's been on the premises there in these nineteen years since you last saw the view, Mr. Fenway?"

"Old servants, myself, my daughter, my cousin Mott, and a great many innocent bystanders in the way of guests. Since 1940, in the summer and autumn, my sister-in-law, her son, Mrs. Grove, and Hilda. Oh — a young Mr. Craddock."

"Relative?"

"Er — no. My nephew is not strong. Craddock more or less looks after him. Clever, intelligent fellow, newspaper fellow once. He's a convalescent himself, but a very active one!"

Gamadge asked: "Is it conceivable, since your brother was interested in this scheme of writing up the family — is it conceivable that he should have removed the picture — carefully, as he thought, and with the intention of having it replaced again —" Fenway was doggedly shaking his head, but Gamadge continued: "In order to show it to artists abroad, you know; to get the best opinions on reproducing it in color."

Fenway said: "He would have consulted me; and he never took it abroad because he never went abroad again; he died here, of a virulent type of pneumonia, not many weeks after I last saw him looking at the book you are looking at now." For Gamadge was turning its pages.

"Well, then!" Gamadge looked up to smile at his host. "We must conclude, if we are to assume that all your assumptions are correct, that the picture left its place in the book after it reached this house, Thursday a week ago."

Fenway started upright in his chair. He looked deeply shocked. "Mr. Gamadge, put that out of your mind. That's impossible."

"But the view is gone, and you reject all

reasons for its having been torn out at Fenbrook."

"What earthly reason could anybody in this house have had for tearing it out? I never dreamed of suggesting that the thing had happened *here*."

"I suppose it's always easier to shift blame upon the past. But motive is easier to distinguish in the present, and there are distinguishable motives for the mutilation if it took place in this room. I needn't point out that there was opportunity; it lay unwrapped and unguarded on that table for more than twenty-four hours, accessible to the household. But perhaps I should except Mrs. Fenway?"

"My sister-in-law only comes downstairs on special occasions, in a chair, carried by two men."

"We'll except her." Gamadge put aside his cigar, and turned the pages of the book of views.

"We must except them all, Mr. Gamadge."

Gamadge looked up at him. "If you say so; and if you say so, we'll drop the whole thing."

After a moment's silence Fenway said: "I beg your pardon; of course we won't. It's an academic discussion, no harm in it. I must abandon the personal point of view. Please go on, Mr. Gamadge."

"There are only one or two points to be

made. If the mutilation of the book occurred here and lately, it may have been done because somebody knew you'd put a value on the print, and is holding it for ransom. I mean you're to offer a reward, and the picture will be found."

Fenway looked actually sick.

"But the reward wouldn't naturally be very great," continued Gamadge, "hardly more than fifty dollars at most, I suppose. The person who would play such a trick as that on you would have to be very hard up."

"And a petty criminal!"

"First offense, perhaps."

"Nobody in the house, not one of the servants — but they're out of the question — need be reduced to such straits. They would come to me."

"There's the ever-curious question of pride or vanity. I *can* steal, to beg I am ashamed."

"Horrible."

"But you won't like me to suggest that the picture may have been torn from your family archives and destroyed to satisfy a personal grudge — against you or your clan."

"If anybody is cherishing a grudge against me or my family, it's always been concealed very well."

Gamadge closed the book of views. "May I take this home with me overnight, Mr.

Fenway? I'd like to look at it more carefully. I'll bring it back when I bring you your Holmes."

Fenway, recalled to his overpowering sense of obligation, assented almost eagerly. "Of course. Of course. But you really mustn't carry all these books — five, Mr. Gamadge, counting your own!"

"I can manage them very well, if I may have a piece of that wrapping paper, and a length of that string."

Gamadge made a neat bundle, but he did not include *Men Working*; when he and Fenway left the library, he had it under his arm.

5

WASTE PAPER

The upper hall, like the lower one, was high and heavily corniced, and ended at the rear with a glassed door; Gamadge supposed that these doors concealed service stairways and landings. He followed his host over sound-absorbent carpeting to the large sitting room which occupied two-thirds of the house front-age, and which contained six people; but only five of them looked up as the two came in. The sixth, a big young man with thick blond hair, sat hunched at a table between the west windows, pencil in hand and eyes fixed on a paper game, until his companion — another young man, but a thin and active one — rose and touched him on the arm. Then he too got up, and stood vaguely and amiably smiling.

Two women, one reclining on a wheeled invalid chair, sat opposite each other, a round table between them, in the bay window. A younger woman and an elderly man shared a little sofa at right angles to the fireplace, which was in the wall to the right of the doorway; there was another door in the east wall, half open; it led to a handsome and luxurious bedroom, and afforded a glimpse of blue-satin furnishings and a flowered carpet.

"I've fulfilled my promise to you all," said Fenway, "and brought you Mr. Gamadge. Here they all are, Mr. Gamadge, eagerly waiting to make your acquaintance. My sister-in-law, Mrs. Fenway."

Gamadge crossed the room to take the hand that she held out to him; a beautiful hand, and a once beautiful woman; beautiful still, if she had not had that drawn and anxious look, a caged look. Middle age had not lined her fair skin, dimmed her bright blue eyes, faded her blond hair; but it had slightly blurred the clear features which must in other days have been modelled like the Psyche's, but on a larger scale; a large-boned woman, and certainly tall. She wore a smart velvet coat, dark-blue, and there was a flame-colored robe over her legs and feet.

She said: "Very, very good of you to take pity on us, Mr. Gamadge. We're so *dull*."

Gamadge, looking into the strained blue eyes, said that he couldn't believe that.

"Poor Mrs. Grove will tell you so. My friend Mrs. Grove, Mr. Gamadge."

Mrs. Grove, a thin, small woman with a

birdlike face, weather-beaten and unreadable, smiled with tight lips and regarded him unsmilingly from small dark eyes. Then she went back to her needlework. The round table was heaped with it — squares of canvas, myriad-colored skeins of crewel wool, scissors, workbags. The telephone which stood there was almost smothered, and a wastebasket under it contained many snippings of worsted. It also contained a crumpled paper ball.

"My daughter," said Fenway. Gamadge turned to acknowledge the short nod vouchsafed him by Miss Fenway. He saw again the dark, plain, well-bred features that he had seen the night before; the fine brown hair, plainly dressed; the clear, colorless skin. She was wearing a tailored suit and a silk blouse, but the brilliant earrings were in her ears, and there was a big sapphire ring on her right hand; old-fashioned; a family ring no doubt. He saw that her eyes were hazel, and that there was a sardonic look about them. She was polite and interested.

"My cousin Mott," said Fenway. The tall old man who had risen from beside Caroline had Fenway's blue eyes, the Fenway short, high nose, and Caroline's sardonic expression; but he lacked the Fenway gravity. He had the humorous look of a tired old man who has found life rather absurd on the whole, and

74

doesn't care. He said: "I've been looking forward to this. Mr. Gamadge, I read you."

"We all do," said Caroline.

"Indeed we do!" Mrs. Fenway smiled, and once it could not have mattered what she said when she smiled. Even now the smile was warming.

"Thank you all very much," said Gamadge.

"My nephew Alden," said Fenway.

Gamadge turned completely to acknowledge this introduction. No, he thought, you wouldn't guess unless you knew. He was vague, but he behaved as any rather stupid young fellow would behave; amiably, indifferently. He nodded, and stood quietly beside his chair. His mother's son, and — if you caught a glimpse of her face when she looked at him — the apple of her eye.

"And Mr. Craddock," said Fenway, "and now we can all sit down."

Craddock, a pale, wiry, black-haired young man with an intelligent face and an air of nervous repressed energy, came forward with a chair; he placed it near Mrs. Fenway, and when Gamadge sat down in it he had the whole group within his range of vision; he was directly facing Caroline. Fenway settled himself opposite her and his cousin Mott, at the other end of the hearth; Craddock returned to the table between the west windows, and he and

Alden returned to their game.

Quite a responsibility, thought Gamadge, for an untrained man; to look after a big fellow like that. If young Fenway wanted to, and knew how, he could break Craddock in two.

"Mr. Gamadge," said Fenway, "has just done me a most tremendous favor. A trade in books, and I'm very much afraid he has the worst of it."

Caroline said, dropping the ash of her cigarette into the fire, "I don't think he's been humoring you, Father."

Gamadge smiled. "You don't think I look like the kind of idiot who'd cheat himself out of politeness?"

"That's cheating the other person."

"You're quite right."

"You don't behave so feebly, I think."

Gamadge laughed. "I'm flattered."

Mott Fenway was amused. He said, removing his cigar to do so, "We're great philosophers here, you observe, Mr. Gamadge; fond of dialectic."

"You needn't make fun of me, you know, Cousin Mott," said Caroline. She added, as Gamadge laid *Men Working* on the table in a spot clear of needle point, "Is that a philosophical book, Mr. Gamadge?"

"Very; and it has a message."

"Oh, dear!" said Mott, in his subhumorous way.

"Definitely a message." Gamadge was by this time so acutely aware of tension in the atmosphere about him that he was afraid he might betray his own nervousness. He went on, respectfully taking in the charming gray, brown and yellow room: "If you'll allow me to say so, the Fenways have a message for moderns. You have the best taste of all — you know what not to change." But he wondered how the Fenways got fabrics replaced when these faded or became threadbare. The gilt-and-walnut furniture had of course been made for eternity.

"We are a little antiquated, I'm afraid," said Fenway. "Aren't we, Belle?"

This seemed to be a family joke. Mrs. Fenway, who had picked up her work again, gave him an affectionate smile. "The awful truth is, Mr. Gamadge," she said, "that when I was first married I teased my dear husband and upset my father-in-law very much by wanting things changed here and at Fenbrook. I wanted art moderne, and I wanted the dreariest kind of decorator's colonial. They finally made me understand that a master had done both houses, and that nothing must ever be altered."

"You were very good for us, my dear," said

Fenway. "At least your great bathroom crusade was a success." He asked suddenly: "Are you sure you and Mrs. Grove want that window open? Don't you feel the draught?"

The middle window of the bay, as Gamadge had noticed, was raised an inch or so. Mrs. Fenway shook her head. "There's no draught, even on the coldest days, and Alice and I are used to old, cold Europe. We sometimes feel a little suffocated in all this lovely steam heat, and with the open fire besides." She added, with a glance at the other, and the faint tone of diffidence that Gamadge had noticed in her voice when she addressed her: "Don't we, Alice?"

Mrs. Grove raised her eyes, smiled faintly, and lowered them again to her work. Her needle went methodically down between rows of diagonal stitches, and then its blunt and shining point reappeared from below.

"My sister-in-law," said Fenway, "is at last graciously permitted to alter something at Number 24. The drawing-room brocade is in rags, the design can't be copied, there are no such colors any more; so she and Mrs. Grove have taken on the stupendous task of working demi-point covers for six side chairs, two armchairs, a bench and a settee. Did you ever see more beautiful patterns?"

Gamadge, leaning forward to pick up a corner of a square, and clumsily pushing a pair of scissors off the table with his cuff, said they were indeed beautiful. Then he apologized, and bent to retrieve the scissors. He also retrieved the paper ball from the wastebasket, palmed it, and rose with it in his left hand and the scissors in his right. He slipped the crumpled paper in his pocket, laid the scissors on the table, and again admired the wreaths and scrolls against their pale-green background.

A rather low, deep voice, coming from somewhere on his extreme right, interrupted him. "My pencil's broken."

"I'll get you one, old man." Craddock rose.

Mrs. Fenway turned her head to look at her son, who sat frowning and regarding his pencil. "Darling," she said, "you mustn't let poor Bill get your pencil for you. Go and get one yourself."

"No, really, Mrs. Fenway; it won't take a second. The kind he likes are up in my room."

Craddock went out into the hall and ran up the stairs to the top floor. Alden sat patiently waiting, his eyes on his pencil; his mother's haunted eyes remained on him — they were full of love and anxiety. A silence ensued, during which Miss Fenway lighted another cigarette, and Mott Fenway whistled under his breath; a cheerful tune it was, from

79

another century. Craddock returned. Blake Fenway went back to the subject of needlework:

"Mrs. Grove's young niece Hilda copied the designs for our new covers at the Metropolitan Museum, Mr. Gamadge; they will be unique."

"That dear child," said Mrs. Fenway. "How she worked over it, and how clever she is. Does all this rather impress you as belonging in the well-known ivory tower, Mr. Gamadge?"

Gamadge said that he liked towers in a landscape.

"Hilda shouldn't be in one, though. I don't know how you can all keep her marooned up there in that barn of a Fenbrook, I'm sure." Mrs. Fenway's tone was light, but she seemed to take the matter seriously; and Craddock, at the mention of the absent Hilda, had raised his head. His dark eyes moved from one speaker to the other, and back again.

"I think myself that it must be lonely for her." Blake Fenway looked perturbed.

"Isn't she supposed to like it there?" Caroline's eyes were on the tip of her cigarette.

"Now, that's nonsense," said Mrs. Fenway cheerfully. "No girl of her age could possibly like it; and I cannot see why the boys at least shouldn't go up for weekends. It's too absurd. Hilda is your secretary, Blake, and the Dobsons are fellow employees; she's part of the staff."

Craddock was heard to mutter that Hilda liked to ski.

"Of course she does. Why shouldn't you all ski?"

Caroline drily remarked that perhaps Mrs. Grove might have an opinion on the subject.

Gamadge heard that lady's voice for the first time. It was a small, dry, clear voice. It said: "I can safely leave the decision to Mr. Fenway."

"Yes." Caroline glanced at her. "And we all know very well what it will be; exactly what it would be if I were nineteen and in Hilda's place. Won't it, Father?"

"Why not, my dear?"

Mrs. Fenway smiled roguishly at Gamadge. "I'm in a minority, it seems. But I'm always on the side of the young people, you know."

Mott Fenway said that it was dusty work for the little girl, sorting out old books and papers; and went on to introduce a subject which Blake Fenway had apparently not intended to discuss with the family that afternoon. "Wonder what else will turn up missing." He looked at the guest. "Mysterious disappearance of a house, Mr. Gamadge."

"Really?"

81

"Picture of our old house, torn out of its book."

"Oh; yes. I saw the place where it had been."

"Was it valuable, do you think?" asked Mrs. Fenway. "Could somebody have got money for it? I mean some unscrupulous guest, of course; if such there ever can have been at Fenbrook!"

"Or the unscrupulous servant of a visiting guest," said Mott.

"Do you think it *could* have been sold for anything much, Mr. Gamadge?" asked Mrs. Fenway.

"The set of books is worth a tidy sum; if you call seventy-five to a hundred dollars a tidy sum," said Gamadge. "I'm only guessing, you know."

"A tidy sum," smiled Mott Fenway.

"The plate alone, no; I should think little or nothing."

Young Craddock said: "I know a fellow who papered a room with them."

"With what?" asked Caroline.

"Old portraits and views. Bought 'em up for five cents apiece, and pasted 'em up. Very nice, unusual."

"Fenbrook wasn't pasted up," smiled Mott. "But we might paste up some of the ancient bills and documents."

"Oh no," protested Mrs. Fenway, closing her eyes. "There's just one thing to do with old papers, and that's to throw them away — throw them away!"

Gamadge shuddered, Fenway shuddered, and Mott sympathetically smiled. Caroline said: "I wish we could get the thing back. I wish Mr. Gamadge would concentrate on it. Then we'll give you something *you* want, won't we, Father? If we have it. Perhaps there's a first edition of somebody up at Fenbrook still."

Gamadge, rising, said that if they came across the Trollope he was looking for, he was in the market.

"What Trollope?" Caroline got out of her chair when the men stood up.

"He Knew He Was Right."

"A grimmer book never was written," said Mott.

"But it has a message!"

Everybody laughed except Craddock and Alden Fenway. Alden had risen when Craddock did, and stood as if amiably waiting for the moment when he could sit down again. Gamadge took Mrs. Fenway's hand.

"It was good of you to let me come up and see you," he said.

"I beg and pray that you'll come again!"

"I shall." Gamadge picked up his novel, and

bowed to Mrs. Grove. Mrs. Grove bowed, Craddock bowed, Alden ducked his head. The three others accompanied the guest out of the room and to the top landing of the stairs.

"I'll take you down," said Mott. "We spare old Phillips."

"For if we wear him out," smiled Caroline, "where shall we find his like again?"

"Ruthless child!" Mott benevolently surveyed her as she stood with her arm through her father's. "She will have no cant in the house. Very uncomfortable for the rest of us, who employ ever so much of it."

Fenway protested: "I only hope that Mr. Gamadge understands your peculiar sense of humor, and Caroline's."

"Oh, I'm sure he does," murmured Caroline.

Gamadge said that there was room in the world at present for an essay on pure candor by Miss Fenway.

Caroline laughed. "I'm sure there isn't. There never was room anywhere for any of my writing, Mr. Gamadge. I've done all of it I'm ever going to do. I stopped that sort of nonsense a long time ago."

"Perhaps you stopped too soon."

"At least I had high hopes once. What was I going to do, Father? Do you remember? Found a salon, or a magazine?"

"My dear, I could never understand why the editors wouldn't have your work."

"After you finished censoring it, darling, it never had a chance."

Those two understood each other; they bade Gamadge farewell, standing arm in arm and smiling, as he went down the stairs with Mott Fenway.

"I could find my own hat and coat, sir, you know," said Gamadge.

"A little deception; I wanted a private word with you." Mott glanced over his shoulder, keenly enough for all his joking manner. "Have you a quarter of an hour?"

"Certainly."

"So private that I don't want the rest of them to know I'm having it. Shall we go to the library? They'll all be upstairs now until teatime."

"I have some books to pick up there." But as they reached the lower hall, and Mott turned towards the darkening end of it, Gamadge paused: "Forgive the suggestion; if they're to think I've gone, wouldn't it be strategy on our part to slam the front door?"

Mott, hands in the pockets of his loose old lounge coat, also stopped. He looked amused. "I'm a child in the hands of the expert. Slam it, by all means."

Gamadge did so. Then he said: "Now perhaps I'd better have my hat and coat. Then, if somebody *should* drop in on us, I could say that I'd forgotten something, and you'd let me in again."

Mott was highly entertained. "I see that I've come to the right shop; presence of mind and subterfuge are what I want, and I think I may be going to find them in you, as well as the intellect I'm already sure of." He opened the door under the stairs, and Gamadge found his possessions among a closetful of outer garments; then they went on down the hall and into the library. Gamadge dropped coat, hat and novel on top of the wrapped parcel of books that he had left on the long table, and turned to face the other. "Well, sir, what can I do for you?"

"It's this matter of the lost view of Fenbrook, Mr. Gamadge. A curious riddle. Let's tackle it sitting down."

"Well, sir —" Gamadge looked at the wide doorway through which they had entered, walked to it, and stationed himself, with a smile, against the left-hand jamb. He spoke amiably: "*You* sit down. I'll keep a lookout."

"Upon my word!"

"You care to run the risk of being overheard?"

"We shouldn't be overheard, Mr. Gamadge, because nobody in the house thinks that there's anything to overhear. Only Caroline knows that I have suspicions, and she doesn't imagine the worst of them."

"If you have suspicions, there must be at least one suspect; a suspect may have an uneasy conscience. I'll stay comfortably here, if it's all the same to you."

"Not quite the same to me as having you opposite me in front of the fire. However, I'm in no position to bully you; I'm about to ask a favor." He moved a chair to face Gamadge, and sat down.

6

HOUSE DIVIDED

The fire had died to red embers. Fenway put out a long, delicate-looking hand towards it, crossed one long leg over the other knee, and contemplated Gamadge thoughtfully. At last he said: "I'm hoping that this may turn out to be a business proposition; if I didn't have that hope I shouldn't have the colossal cheek to take up your time."

"Very glad to be of service, if I can be."

"I myself, of course, have no money at all. I'm a pauper, the clothes on my back and the loose change in my pocket provided for me by my cousin Blake. You will guess the sort of person he is when I say that neither of us ever thinks of the obligation. But *I* can't pay your doubtless high fees. However, I can promise you that Caroline will, if you're inclined to help us."

"Let me understand you, Mr. Fenway. Has Miss Fenway asked you to consult me about the plate that was torn out of the book of views?"

"Good Heavens, no; she doesn't dream that I'm consulting you. I didn't think of doing so until I had had a chance to — er — study you a little this afternoon. Your books prepared me to find you very competent, but one cannot always judge a man's — er — code of manners from the books he writes, can one?"

Gamadge said, laughing, that one certainly could not.

"There is a certain disloyalty to Blake, of course, in taking you into my confidence; or would be if I didn't feel that I could trust you with a lot of family stuff that Blake would never confide to anybody. He's very reticent, sensitive, clannish, you know. I have told you what I owe my cousin, or part of what I owe him. I've known him since he was born — I knew Cort — and we have the same background and the same memories. But I am not —" he smiled — "in the best Fenway tradition, as you see. However: there is Caroline to be considered too. One can always tell whether young people resent one's presence in a house or not."

"Yes."

"Caroline has always wanted me here and at Fenbrook. We are in sympathy, we get on; we have more in common, I'm afraid, than she and her father have, devoted though they are. She gave up a good deal to be with him, you know — her own independent life. I owe her something, and in doing what I'm doing now I am serving her. If we find that picture, Mr. Gamadge, she'll pay your bill — anything you care to ask. She hasn't her own fortune yet, won't have it until her father dies, but she has a certain amount of money from her mother, and could get more."

Gamadge said: "This kind of investigation is really a hobby of mine, Mr. Fenway; I'm not a licensed detective, I have no facilities, and I can't promise results. If I could manage to be of assistance to you and Miss Fenway I shouldn't dream of taking money for the job."

"But you must be an extremely busy man; why should you come to the assistance of comparative strangers for nothing?"

"Well, I like a puzzle."

"That is fortunate for us. If I'm to put this one fairly before you, I must begin with those indiscretions I hinted at. Perhaps you don't need to be told that this household is divided into two camps?"

Gamadge looked enquiring.

"Surely you noticed that Caroline and I — and Blake too, though he won't admit it — get more enjoyment out of a guest like yourself when we have him to ourselves?"

90

"In the upper hall?" Gamadge smiled.

"Exactly so. Blake is really in our camp — Caroline's and mine; or I should say that we are really both in hers. But his consideration for others makes him practically a neutral, and he is not and could not be a party to our conspirings."

Gamadge said: "It's a large house."

"It is, and there's no reason why we shouldn't all live comfortably enough in it, going our separate ways; but Blake cannot bear to feel that his sister-in-law should be left out of things and forsaken. All this must come oddly from me, since I'm a hanger-on myself." He paused, and looked at Gamadge.

"No, I understand; you're of their blood, and all the rest of it."

"Yes. As for me, I can get on with anybody and put up with anything; that's one of my few virtues, the virtue of a professional dependent. But it's hard on Caroline."

"I can see that it might be."

"Might be? My dear Mr. Gamadge! Caroline gave up her separate life, and what might have been something of a career, to preside in her father's house. For two and a half years Belle Fenway has been in the house with her afflicted son and her entourage. Wherever Belle Fenway happens to be, she will always impose her personality; she can't help it. She's always had an establishment of her own until now, and she sometimes forgets that she isn't the mistress of this one. Invalided, confined to her rooms upstairs, she dominates us.

"And it all came about so naturally; Blake asked her to come here until she was able to take Alden to a house or an apartment — they're of course well able to afford anything; the poor fellow is a rich man. She won't be separated from him — that's natural enough too, though I think it's a great mistake on her part, both for his sake and her own. By the way, I'm assuming that you are aware of his affliction."

"It's not obvious."

"Poor Blake thinks it's invisible, and Belle, of course, is never so happy as when she can persuade herself that Alden is a normal member of society. Well, we have them here, we have the enigmatic Mrs. Grove, we have Craddock — a young fellow who is as well equipped to deal with a patient like Alden Fenway as I am — and we have, or had, Hilda Grove. A very nice child indeed, I am quite fond of her, but a fifth outsider. Five is a good many."

"It is."

"Belle's injury is slower in healing than the doctors at first expected; some nerve was involved, I think. Alden is a perpetual source of — we'll say awkwardness; he's a spiritual depressant. It isn't generally known, by the way, even now, that there's anything wrong with him, but it's bound to leak out. Rather a blight on a house.

"Mind you, if there were no more to it than that, I should strongly advise Caroline — as I have advised her in the past — to seek grace and say nothing; to keep things smooth and comfortable for her father. But now — it's a responsibility. I've known certain disturbing things for some time now, suspected others; Caroline's begun to feel that something's wrong in the other camp. She's getting very nervous.

"I'll go back to the first incident, which I wasn't over-much perturbed about at the time; two years ago Caroline's dog was found dead in the street."

Gamadge had been thoughtfully smoking. Now he looked up, startled.

"Nice fellow, a Dalmatian," continued Mott Fenway. "She'd only had him down here in New York for a month. Some ear trouble, needed long treatment at a vet's. Well-mannered dog, we were all fond of him; he did no senseless barking. Had the run of the yard and lawn all day, but was kept indoors at night; his bed was in a lobby off the basement hall. One morning he was found with his head crushed, in the gutter opposite the service door; you know it? Door in the wall."

Gamadge nodded.

"Everybody said he'd been struck by a car, and everybody thought that old Phillips had forgotten to lock him in the night before, and had also left the service door open. He's as likely, by the way, to leave the front door open; but there seemed no other explanation, and Phillips didn't defend himself from the imputation with any great violence; he'd scorn to. He denied it, and that was the end of that.

"I must now explain that my room is a northwest one, on the top floor. Craddock has the northeast corner, and there are a bath and a long clothes closet between us. I'm in the habit of sitting up late to read, and one night, about a year ago, I sat up unconscionably late over a good book. When I opened my west window — it overlooks the yard, and I seldom do open it at night, I don't like to be waked by milkmen and the rest of it — I saw an exodus. Don't ask me who it was that flitted through the service door; the yard is as dark as pitch in the dim-out.

"Well; I've already said that I mind my own business, and I'm not the man to lose sleep spying out of a window. I made a few eliminations, of course; the servants? You should see them; their midnight excursions — after-

94

midnight excursions, it was two o'clock — have long ceased. Burglar? We have an alarm, which must have been switched off indoors. The possibilities reduced themselves to young Craddock and Mrs. Grove.

"I dismissed Mrs. Grove as unlikely in the highest degree. I did not knock on the communicating door to Craddock's room; first because he was not then — is not yet, in fact — a well man, and I didn't care to risk waking him; next, because I rather sympathized with him. His must be a dull, a deadly life; I didn't find it in my heart to grudge him a little irregular amusement.

"Next morning I thought of the dog; ugly, very ugly, but a conjecture. Should I, on the strength of the conjecture, talk to Blake, upset him fearfully, upset Belle Fenway and Mrs. Grove, enrage Craddock to the point of making him throw up the job?

"We know nothing about him, of course, except what Mrs. Grove has told us — that he comes of decent people and had a newspaper job in China. He's fond of Hilda, but Blake rather quashed that; the boy is in no position to support a wife, Hilda Grove isn't trained to support herself, and even Blake didn't see his way to supporting a war bride; Craddock will be in one or other of the services, of course, as soon as he's able. Blake suggested that a recognized affair would be, as things were and are, no advantage to the girl; and I must say that she herself seems quite passive in the matter.

"Craddock has been a godsend to those two women — Mrs. Grove and Belle Fenway; he got them home — with Belle injured and Alden a dead weight, got them through all the hardships of a frightful voyage, and is now supposedly the person best qualified to look after Alden as Belle wants him looked after — tactfully, discreetly, and so on. He's a treasure. They'd fight me tooth and nail if I made trouble for him. I didn't do anything about it, and no doubt that fact is enough to explain my present circumstances and myself."

Mott sat back in his chair and got out a cigarette. "But now the case is altered. Whether or not Craddock killed the dog, his excursions at night (I suppose there were more than one) prove that he's not to be trusted they also indicate that he's capable of neglecting his job in other ways. Caroline and I think that the view of Fenbrook was torn out of the book after it arrived here, torn out by that unfortunate boy; we think he may be turning mischievous, and perhaps destructive, and conceivably dangerous. And Craddock didn't — perhaps doesn't — take him seriously enough to stay on the job at night."

Gamadge looked at the other. "Any proof?"

"About the view? None whatever, but we can't account for the wantonness of the mutilation in any other way. Belle would deny the possibility; she'll call the specialists in again, and they may back her up. They swore this kind of case never progressed into violence or even surliness; and Belle says that Fagon's treatments were only to prevent deterioration, and to teach him to take care of himself and make a good showing. He does, I must say. I've never seen him anything but amiable. But the experts may be wrong; and if they are, and this tearing out of the picture is a sign that they're wrong, is Craddock the sort of person to notice danger signals?

"One more thing; since the discovery that the view was lost — a week ago Friday, I believe — Caroline says that she has noticed strain and anxiety in the other camp. She says it's quite obvious, and she thinks that Belle and Mrs. Grove know who tore the picture out of the book, and are hiding the knowledge for fear that Alden will be sent away."

Gamadge said: "That's interesting."

"She thinks Alden's hidden the thing, and that they can't find it. She's sure that somebody's been looking for something through the house at night. If Belle or Mrs. Grove — or Craddock, if he knows what's up — could find the thing, and destroy it, there'd be no proof against Alden."

"What proof would there be in any case?"

"He may have marked it up in some way; he's always scribbling. He can't play that game — noughts and crosses — but he uses up a dozen sheets of paper at it every day."

"Why should he tear that particular view out of that particular book?"

"Craddock or Mrs. Grove had plenty of time to show it to him; either of them may have told him great tales of the family grandeur. He's the male heir, you know." Mott Fenway's expression combined satire with sadness. "He may have thought it was something he ought to own."

Gamadge smoked thoughtfully. "You and Miss Fenway have built up something of a case."

Mott's eyes, hooded by wrinkled lids like a big bird's, creased at the corners; he smiled. "Our motives are mixed. Caroline is frankly nervous; but what it really amounts to is that if we can find the picture ourselves, and prove that Alden tore it out of the book, we'll get rid of the whole tribe of them."

Gamadge smiled a little too. "Will you?"

"Of course. Alden will go. If he can do a thing like that, Blake won't have him in the house; what mayn't he do next? Belle will go with him, Mrs. Grove with her, and Craddock will be out of a job. I suppose," he added slowly, "that it will be the end of that child up at Fenbrook; I mean, as far as the Fenways are concerned. But I think she won't mind learning a job. I shall miss her, though. . . . The aunt's rather grim."

"I thought so too."

"Well, there you have it." Mott gestured with the hand that held the cigarette. "A situation that for all we know may be dangerous, and one that we think depends on finding a picture. We can't find it, they can't find it; could you?"

"Is that my assignment?" Gamadge raised his eyebrows.

"That's your assignment. Those books of yours — you have found things, you know how other people have found things."

"I have been lucky at that game. But you said that somebody else was prowling about the house at night; shouldn't I run into the prowler?"

Mott Fenway had not really believed that Gamadge would consent to do more than advise him; he did not attempt to disguise his pleasure and surprise: "You'll actually consider helping us?"

"Not if it means being discovered and thrown out."

"I shouldn't dream of letting you in for that; been thinking it over very carefully." Mott leaned forward, punctuating his remarks with jabs of his cigarette. "The thing is to look when nobody else is looking; when nobody is paying any attention to empty rooms. Right after dinner."

"But you didn't invent that notion, Mr. Fenway; the second-story men did."

"All our windows are fastened, of course. I'll let you in by the service door and the basement, say at nine o'clock. The servants will be busy in their own working quarters, and we'll go up by the back stairs. They lead straight up to the top floor, and I can keep you in my own room till the coast is clear. I don't think anybody will be going anywhere tonight; Blake and Caroline will be in the sitting room, or if Caroline isn't, she'll be in her own bedroom, or perhaps at the piano downstairs. If we run into her she won't betray us, I can promise you. I haven't told her anything about this plan of mine — better leave her out of it; but she won't betray us. I'll go around with you, do the scouting. When you see the arrangement of rooms and back stairs you'll understand how easy it is."

"Where will Craddock be?"

"In the sitting room. What happens is this: Blake and I and Caroline have our coffee there with the others; then Blake and I go down to the library and have a quiet cigar, and then he or I may or may not invite Craddock to a game of billiards; we have a billiard and game-room in the basement. Caroline sometimes joins us if she's at home. More usually, Blake goes up and takes a hand of bridge with Belle, Mrs. Grove and Craddock. Sometimes Caroline or I cut in. Now I can pretty well direct operations; I'll be too lazy for billiards, I'll get Blake settled at bridge by nine o'clock. Unless we're very unlucky, we'll have the house to ourselves."

"How are the rooms arranged?"

"Belle's is the corner one next the sitting room; Mrs. Grove's is next hers, with a bath between. Alden's is next Mrs. Grove's, at the south end of the house. Blake's suite is opposite, and Caroline has her room and her bath beyond him, next the sitting room on the west."

"Do you suggest that I shall find the view in a couple of hours?"

"It wouldn't be in any bedroom but Alden's, and probably not in his."

"And you think tonight would be a good night for a paper chase?"

"The sooner the better. Blake said that you might be going away. It's a sporting proposition, Gamadge; you might have luck. I really cannot tell you what it would mean to me — to get that picture back for my cousin, and perhaps to be able to tell Caroline — oh, ridiculous." He sat back. "Ridiculous to make a sentimental appeal to you. Why should you care about all this?"

"It's a sporting proposition, as you say; and I assure you I'd very much like to know that Mr. Fenway had his picture back."

"Of course you'd appreciate him."

"It's a forlorn hope, in the circumstances. Even if I knew the picture were in the house I couldn't promise results in the time."

Mott Fenway was looking pleased and alert. "It's uncommonly good of you. I shouldn't dream of asking such a favor if I didn't think there might be more serious developments later on."

Gamadge's attitude now changed; he put out his cigarette, and addressed Fenway with the air of a man taking over a job. "I'll have to let you know when to be expecting me at the door in the wall. How about telephoning you?"

"There's a telephone just outside this room. I'll be here until you call me."

"But the switch may be on upstairs; I mustn't announce myself. I'll give the name of Hendrix, and say something about an appointment for tomorrow. What shall it be?"

102

Mott was amused. "Someone at the Vernon club wants a bridge game."

"Good. But suppose I broke a leg or was suddenly prevented in some other way from getting to a telephone?"

"I sincerely hope not!"

"You'd have to be notified. If anybody else calls you in the name of Hendrix, it will be one of my operatives."

Fenway stared.

"And if the name of Hendrix comes up later, in any other connection, you must play up. Research takes one far afield, and mine may lead me into byways. Mr. Hendrix is the name of the son of one of your classmates. What university?"

Mott Fenway, looking dazed, murmured: "Harvard."

"You know all about Mr. Hendrix, son of your old Harvard classmate. Or —" Gamadge laughed — "would you prefer to know nothing about him at all? I ought to have warned you; when I interest myself in a case, or what looks as if it might turn out to be a case, I become unpredictable. I mean that I follow all leads, and I go on following them. Shall we call the whole thing off?"

Fenway met the greenish eyes of this genie whom he appeared to have released from its bottle. He said: "Certainly not. I can trust you

103

not to distress my cousin Blake and Caroline, and not to get us into the papers."

"And may I suggest that you ought not to take the opposition too lightly? You suspect Craddock of having killed a dog so that it shouldn't bark when he deserted his post at night. You suspect three people in this house of keeping what may be a dangerous secret from Mr. Blake Fenway. You think Mrs. Fenway has no scruples where the comfort of her son is concerned. You may be quite wrong about it all, but if I were in your place I shouldn't care to be overheard discussing it."

Mott Fenway smiled. "None of those people would dream of suspecting me of conspiracy against them, Mr. Gamadge. What you don't quite realize is my unimportance — to them. I'm a good-natured nonentity, hardly a person at all."

"If I can't impress *you* with the importance of being discreet, let me appeal to you on behalf of Miss Fenway. You don't want her to incur the ill will of unscrupulous persons?"

Fenway rose. "Caroline is very careful. I dare say you're quite right to be concerned about us, and I'm obliged to you; but I have walked on eggs for many years, and I think I have learned the art. I don't allow her to be uncivil upstairs."

Gamadge thought that Miss Fenway had once or twice come rather close to incivility upstairs. He said: "Whatever these people have or haven't done, you propose to dislodge them all from a security they've enjoyed for more than two years."

"My dear young man, I'm sorry to have frightened you on my account. I'll really be careful."

Gamadge went and put on his coat; hat in one hand, his books under the other arm, he went out and down the hall. Fenway accompanied him to the front door. Leaning into the vestibule, his gray hair blowing about his forehead, he whispered: "I'll say I had a look at the weather." He withdrew, and the front door closed after him with a thunderous slam.

7

FIRST ARROW

The upper windows of Number 24 commanded a long prospect to the north, south and east; Gamadge therefore hurried west, to enter the nearest drugstore. He explored his pocket for the paper ball which he had rescued from the wastebasket, and unrolled it carefully. It proved to be nothing but the Sunday section of a local timetable, with a pencilled arrow marking Rockliffe Station on the Hudson. His watch said 4:30; there was a train for Rockliffe at 5:30, arriving at 5:46. He entered a booth, made a telephone call, and then dashed from the store and hailed a taxi. He was at the Grand Central in time to check his parcel of books at the package office.

Harold joined him at the gate one minute before the train left. The sergeant wore his trousers tucked into his high boots, and carried a pair of obsolete galoshes under his arm. He said, as they walked down the ramp: "These things nearly lost me the train. Where are we going to, and why are we dressing up like Eskimos?"

"Rockliffe. That's the station for Fenbrook, and Fenbrook is up on top of a hill — and what a hill! I don't believe the snowploughs make it."

They found an end seat in the last car, behind a party consisting of a hatless woman, a baby, and a boy of six.

"They don't look as if they'd take much interest in our conversation," said Gamadge, "but we'd better not use names. Names carry, and on these locals you never know; lady in front might be a friend of the wife of a gardener."

He struggled into his arctics, and the train moved. Harold asked: "You've seen this place?"

"No, only the front entrance to it, which is on the Albany road. The house is buried in trees."

"Does the family climb that hill you were telling about every time they go up for a weekend?"

"Oh, no; they get out at the next station this side of Rockliffe, and drive — or taxi. We're going informally, leaving no trail behind us; straight as the goat climbs from Rockliffe station, I think. There used to be a private road, I remember seeing it from the trains. That was before the station was called Rockliffe, you know; it used to be Fenway Landing, with a private boathouse and a pier. The Fenway property went down to the river; I often used to see the old piles and timbers of the landing, rotting away. But the lower land was sold, the Fenways lost their local importance, and the new station was called Rockliffe after a political chateau on the heights."

"What are we going for?"

"I don't know; I'm following instructions." Gamadge handed the marked timetable to Harold. "Sunday section — that meant that I was to take the trip today, come wind come weather."

"The client slipped you this?"

Gamadge told Harold the story of the afternoon in detail; when he had finished they had passed Morris Heights.

Harold said: "Not much doubt who the client is. What a setup! Crippled woman, and her son can't even be trusted to carry messages for her. You think she could slip her hand out of that open middle window, and drop the paper ball, without the other woman seeing her do it?"

"Easily. The table's between, and they'd lean over to get the light on their work; hundreds of colors to match, some of them off-whites and grays. And that needle-point work

108

— you ever see it being done? They put their hands under when they bring the needle up for the next stitch. Big squares of canvas — perfect cover."

"What a setup. She was all ready for you."

"She might have another message for me if she only knew I was going back there tonight."

Harold smiled. "That's why you are going back — not to look for any picture."

"I'm going to try to report on this trip. It's a godsend — this chance to get into the house."

"Just so long as the old gentleman is O.K."

"What do you mean, O.K.?"

Harold, after a pause, asked a question instead of answering Gamadge's. "You're sure you didn't leave anything out? Gave me the whole thing just as it happened?"

"You know as much as I do; you can get what I got," said Gamadge, "if your mind works the way mine does."

"You did get something?"

"Nothing to talk about yet. How about you? You look as if you had ideas."

"I'm thinking about motive."

"I wasn't, but I'd be glad to have your opinion on the subject."

"The companion, with the young feller she got hold of to look after young F. — they're

109

blackmailing Mrs. F. about something the boy's done; something a darned sight more serious than tearing a picture out of a book. He did tear it out, but the blackmail is about something that would create a big scandal, perhaps bring the police in."

Gamadge looked interested.

"It's the only explanation," continued Harold. "It all fits in. They're bleeding Mrs. F. of every cent she gets paid by the estate for her upkeep and the boy's; that's why she can't leave Number 24. She hasn't anything left to live on."

"How about the lost picture? Miss F. noticed signs of unrest up in that sitting room shortly after the book of views came into the house; the first message the client threw out of the window seems to have been thrown out the day after the book came. That lost picture is what started all the trouble."

"The boy did tear it out, and if it's found it's more evidence against him. Mrs. G. and C. are holding it over the client's head; *she* doesn't want you to find it. She's never given you any instructions about finding a picture. Naturally the blackmailers won't want you to find it — it would bust up the game. They're using it to put the screws on her; she can't raise enough money for them, and she's desperate."

110

"Desperate indeed." Gamadge looked out of the window at the dark river flowing between its icy banks. "Why was I called in?"

"Well, that's the catch."

"It is indeed. What am I to do for my client?"

"She hasn't let you in on the blackmail scheme because she thinks you might not want to help her about this bad break the son made."

"She's running a risk; she must know that I may find out about it."

"Perhaps she thinks you'd keep quiet; it may be something that would look worse to the family and the law than it would to you."

"Hopes I'd condone it?"

"The poor guy didn't mean any harm."

"Let's say she thinks I won't find out about that. What, I repeat, does she want me to do up at this house we're going to?"

"Well, in the first place, the girl's kept up there by the aunt so she won't catch on to what's happening at Number 24. She's a nice kind of girl, by what they all say. Didn't you tell me the client seemed more interested in her than the aunt was?"

"The aunt showed very little interest."

"If the girl was at Number 24 she'd be right on top of them, much closer than Miss F. is, and even Miss F. noticed that something was wrong. Perhaps you're being sent up to get something from Miss G. that would show up Mrs. G. and young C. — make them clear out in a hurry."

"The girl and Mr. C. are supposed to be fond of each other."

"But he's the fondest, isn't he? That's what I gathered from what you said. Anyway, this girl may not know she knows anything. You're to draw the conclusions."

"Even my trusting client can't expect me to work in a void."

"I don't know how it could be more of a void than it is now." Harold frowned. "In your place I couldn't have helped busting the show up this afternoon."

"My client doesn't want it busted up. She's in a vise, and if I turn the wrong screw I may destroy her."

"How are you to turn any screw at all? How are you even going to get into the house up here? How are you going to keep the visit a secret from the other people at Number 24? The first time they telephone, or the girl telephones, she'll tell them we came." He added morosely: "Unless we're climbing in through a window, and I don't want to do that much; I'm in uniform."

"We'll ring the bell. I'm to be a Mr. Hendrix, and the old gentleman will back me up."

"Yes, and that's where I get back to my original question. Is he O.K., or is he a member of the gang?"

Gamadge stared. "A member of the gang?"

"He hasn't got a cent, and all this talk of his about being so grateful —"

"He meant every word of it."

"Just keep your mind open about the people in that house. Say he's one of the blackmailers, and thought it was funny you turned up just now; he's a bright old guy, you say; he's realized you practically invited yourself. He knows you've investigated crimes. Suppose he kept his eye on you this afternoon, and saw you pick that timetable out of the wastebasket. He knew what you meant by those signals — *Men Working* and all the rest of it. When you accepted his invitation for this evening, which was nothing but a test, he knew you were after something."

Gamadge shook his head. "Nobody in the house except my client knows why I went there today. Take that as fact."

"In your place I wouldn't go through that door in the wall tonight or any other night. How about if you were knocked on the head the way that dog was? You'd be thrown in the street, another dim-out fatality."

"I should be more worried about Mott than

about myself if we'd had a chance of being overheard while we discussed Mr. Hendrix in the library. The old gentleman's inclined to underrate the opposition, and I couldn't base any warning on my special knowledge of the case. I didn't dare; my first duty is to my client. But I made certain that we shouldn't be overheard. I stood in the doorway. Nobody came down after we did; I had a good view of the stairs, and of the door at the end of the hall that cuts off the back stairs. I'm afraid I did startle the old thing by suggesting that Mr. Hendrix might pursue other lines of enquiry."

"Come up here, you mean? You hadn't seen the arrow on the timetable when you talked to him."

"I should have come up here in any case. The young lady we're calling on is the only member of the household I hadn't met; of course I meant to get a look at her and at her surroundings."

Harold said after a moment: "I don't think much of Miss F. Her aunt gets turned out of her home in Europe, half-witted son to take care of, gets injured — perhaps for life. You'd think Miss F. would be willing to put up with the situation for a while."

"I can see her point of view."

"Her father's point of view strikes me as

114

the right one. He must be an unusual kind of feller."

"He is. I'd like him to get his picture back."

"You won't find it."

"Not without information from Miss Grove," said Gamadge, as the opened door behind them let in a covering blast of sound, as well as a blast of icy air. The brakeman wailed: "Rockliffe."

It was a tiny station, landscape-gardened in summer, but now swept by all the freezing winds from the northwest. Stars were out in an indigo sky, a yellow afterglow was fading along the black rampart of the Palisades. Gamadge and his assistant climbed the road from the station to a broad and deserted thoroughfare; trolley rails lay like dark threads on the snow.

"Funny without any traffic," said Harold.

They crossed the River Road and attacked the steep grade of what looked like a forest trail. The deep snow, hardly rutted, was banked in high drifts to right and left; shrouded evergreens hid any view of the hillside. At first lights blinked from invisible dwellings, then dusk invaded the lane. Harold got out his torch.

They ploughed on and up in silence. At last

Harold's torch showed a thinning of trees, and beyond them a ravine; the road curved to the left and forked.

"We'll try the left branch," said Gamadge. "The other one probably goes straight on to the Albany Road."

The left branch looked like a private way. It led them, between thickly planted trees, to the untrodden wastes of lawn and garden; no path was distinguishable. They found a route among trees to a semicircular driveway, and stood looking up at the tall front of a brick house painted gray. Pointed trees crowded behind it, and no light showed.

"So this is Fenbrook?" Harold spoke in muted tones, without pleasure.

"It must be; anyhow, I see brackets." Gamadge surveyed the square porch and its ornamental woodwork.

"It's terrible."

"Think so? It's the other chromo — *Life In The Country*. It needs lighted windows."

"We'll never see lights in these windows. The people in there all froze to death a week ago."

But Gamadge mounted two steps and rang an old-fashioned bell. Presently the fanlight and sidelights of the gray door showed yellow, and the door opened. A cheerful-looking fat woman in a cardigan sweater peeped out.

"Is Mr. Mott Fenway at home?" asked Gamadge.

"Oh dear! The family's in New York, sir." The fat woman looked at Gamadge's galoshes, and then past him for a conveyance. She said: "I'm afraid you've had your walk for nothing."

"And what a walk."

"You didn't come up from Rockliffe Station, sir? Oh dear."

"I'm afraid Sergeant Bantz and I have been rather stupid, Mrs. — this *is* Mrs. Dobson?"

"Yes, sir."

"Of course I've heard of you; my name's Hendrix, and I promised Mr. Mott Fenway that I'd drop in sometime when I was in the neighborhood. I happened to be more or less in the neighborhood, and the sergeant is bound for the Oaktree Inn. He thinks it's open."

"Oh yes, sir; and it's only half a mile down the road."

"We found ourselves on Rockliffe Station, which is no place at present to wait for a train. Of course we realize now that we ought to have waited and got out at the next stop, and taxied back. I thought the sergeant might be allowed to telephone for a taxi here, but now I'll call one for us both, if you'll allow me. I'll go on to New York."

Mrs. Dobson looked distressed. "Please

117

come in, and the sergeant too. Miss Grove is here — she'll want to see any friend of the family."

They entered a high, square lobby panelled in red mahogany. Stairs rose from it, and some distance beyond it a swing-door was propped open. A delicious odor of ham frying filled the hall.

Mrs. Dobson closed the front door. "Please excuse the smell of cooking," she said. "I keep the back doors open to warm the front for Miss Grove. We're saving heat while the family's away. If you'll just lay your things on that bench, I'll light the fire in the drawing room."

"Don't bother, Mrs. Dobson."

"It's no bother, sir. I'd be lighting it in a minute or so for Miss Grove."

She went into a room on the right, and turned on a lamp. By the time they had got out of their coats and removed their overshoes a fire was blazing. They entered a big room, also panelled in red mahogany. Mrs. Dobson invited them to the hearth.

"You must be frozen," she said, with a fond glance at Harold's uniform, "and half dead from that climb. Did you say Mr. Mott Fenway, sir?"

"I'm the son of an old Harvard friend of his."

"And what a lovely gentleman he is. He used to pelt snowballs at me when I was a child around the house. My father was coachman here, and my mother was cook. Long ago."

She went out of the room and down the hall. Harold, warming himself, looked about him at the Fenbrook drawing room. He said: "Not so bad. Not so bad. I like the little railings on the furniture. What's the color of those curtains?"

"Peachblow."

"This place was fixed to last."

"It has a permanent look."

"Dressy for a country house."

"Oh, no. They'd put the room into chintz for the summer."

"You were right about it, Mr. Hendrix. It's a good kind of house."

"We had one once."

There was a rush of feet on the stairs, and then a girl came to the doorway. She stood looking at them and smiling. Slim, but strongly built; dark hair rolling back from a low forehead, eyes a shade lighter, the color of brown amber; a clear skin, red-flushed; features that gave the effect of having been carved too finely from delicate material. They gave her, in spite of her obvious health and high spirits, a plaintive look; Gamadge thought of drawings in red or brown chalk, under glass, in museums. Her green knitted dress was faded, her brown shoes had seen long service.

"I'm Hilda Grove, Mr. Hendrix," she said.

Gamadge came forward. "May I introduce Sergeant Bantz, Miss Grove? I don't know him at all, but I think you'll like him."

Miss Grove shook hands with Gamadge and with Harold. She said: "I think it's awful — your both climbing the hill and finding nobody but the Dobsons and me on top of it. Let's all sit down."

They all sat down. Gamadge said: "We really mustn't stay. I'd better be telephoning — I must get to New York. Utterly stupid of me to think the family would be here, transportation being what it is just now. I had some wandering thoughts about the weekend, I suppose, this being Sunday."

"Mr. Fenway — both the Mr. Fenways — will be sick about it."

"I only know Mr. Mott."

"Isn't he nice? But they're all so nice. Mr. Hendrix — *must* you and the sergeant go away before supper? It's frightfully early, but mine's all ready, and Mrs. Dobson says there's plenty of everything. She does so want you both to stay, if you don't mind ham and eggs."

120

Gamadge said: "I had no notion it was so late."

"Oh, it isn't; it's only six-twenty."

"And I must get a train that will reach New York before nine."

"There's one just after eight. You'll have lots of time for supper."

"If you and Mrs. Dobson actually mean it, Miss Grove —" Gamadge looked at Harold — "and the sergeant and I have the colossal nerve —"

Harold said: "I have if you have."

She rose. "Then I'll tell Mrs. Dobson, and Mr. Dobson will show you the downstairs dressing room. You might like to call your taxi now, there's a telephone in the coatroom. The taxis are rather slow sometimes, and when it's snowy everybody wants one."

She went out of the room with a backward glance of pure delight. The two stood silent. At last Harold asked: "Is she or isn't she good-looking?"

Gamadge threw him a glance of mingled pity and disgust.

"Anyway," continued Harold, "she's O.K. So is Mrs. Dobson."

"Yes, and that fixes you, Sergeant. You'll spend the night at the Oaktree Inn."

"What for?"

"I don't know. I must get further instructions. But if I go back to New York you'll have to stay within walking distance of Fenbrook."

"What's this Oaktree Inn, and do they sell toothbrushes?"

"It's a place on the Albany Road, very expensive. I've often passed it in the car. We'll call up and get you a room. You can taxi down to the village with me and buy yourself what you need."

Harold muttered that he would probably need flannel pyjamas.

8

NOT LONELY

An apple-cheeked man in a high pair of rubber boots came shyly to the door. He introduced himself as Dobson, and conducted the guests to the coatroom under the stairs where the telephone was. A well-appointed dressing room opened from it. While Harold washed, Gamadge looked up the 8:01 train to New York, and then ordered a taxi to meet it. He next engaged a room at the Oaktree Inn for Sergeant Bantz; the Oaktree seemed pleasantly surprised.

Harold came out of the dressing room drying his hands. He said it was a crime.

"What is?"

"Eating here under a false name, and telling all these whoppers to that girl. You'll feel pretty small when she and the Dobsons find out that we were here under false pretenses."

"If they ever do find out, they'll have reason to forgive me."

"I'm beginning to think you got your signals wrong. There's nothing for me to do up here."

"You hang on till further notice. I'll keep in touch with you."

When they went out into the hall again Mrs. Dobson met them, beaming. She said: "I'm glad you're going to stay, sir and Sergeant. It's company for the young lady."

"Lonely for her, is it, with the family away?"

"She don't say so, and in good weather it ain't so bad. She keeps out of doors a good deal, she works in the garden. But we've been snowed in."

Gamadge had a suspicion that this was being said in the hope that it would reach Fenway ears. He told Mrs. Dobson that he agreed with her that it must be a dull life for a young person.

"And all that bother about the picture being lost out of the book. We don't know anything about the picture, or the book either."

"A picture has been lost?"

"Twenty years ago, perhaps, and Miss Grove has only been sorting the books and papers for a couple of weeks. But Mr. Fenway don't blame us, of course. It's hard for her to have all the responsibility, though, and no-body to help her. It isn't as if she had friends here; she was brought up in foreign cities, with winter sports on the Alps and I don't know what all. She has no young friends at all in this country. There's no kinder, nicer lady than Miss Caroline, but she don't understand, she has so many friends of her own."

Gamadge smiled at Mrs. Dobson. "I'll drop a word to Mr. Mott Fenway when I see him. I won't quote you, you know."

"Well, sir, I'd be obliged if you wouldn't; it's none of my business. Miss Grove would like to learn how to be a real secretary somewhere, or do war work; but Mrs. Grove won't let anything interfere with Mr. Blake Fenway's plans, and I don't wonder. Still, this isn't like a real job, sir, where you're independent and meet other young people."

Gamadge was quite sure that Mrs. Dobson was no idle gossip, and that it had cost her something to risk her standing with the Fenways in order to put Hilda Grove's case before him. That he had been chosen as intermediary did not surprise him; he was used to the role.

"I see the point," he said.

"She's in the dining room, sir; you go through the parlor."

The dining room was beamed and wainscoted in oak; two corner cupboards rose to the ceiling, whence descended a bronze chandelier. Hilda stood in front of an oak buffet, her hands behind her, contemplating a bottle. She had changed into a lavender dress; it was a summer dress, and it was old. Its thin draperies of skirt and bodice made her look taller, younger and more fragile. Gamadge said from the doorway: "Rossetti never came within a thousand miles of them but once."

"Of whom?" she asked, looking at him in surprise.

"Of the old masters."

"When did he?"

"When he drew that head I'm thinking of. Excuse me — my mind wanders. Is that a bottle of whiskey?"

"Mrs. Dobson says it's what Mr. Fenway would give you."

"Then he's a gentleman."

"There's ice. Would you and Sergeant Bantz fix it yourselves?"

Five minutes later they were all sitting at the oval dinner table; Mrs. Dobson passed ham and eggs and a green salad, and Miss Grove poured coffee.

"It's so lucky," she said. "Mr. Dobson only drinks tea. Where were you stationed, Sergeant Bantz, if it's all right for me to ask?"

Harold swallowed. "An island," he said, after the mouthful went down.

"I've tried him on that," said Gamadge, "and I warn you that that's all you'll get out of him. He won't talk about anything but some kind of monkey."

"Nice little feller," said Harold.

"Are you going to be in this neighborhood long?" asked their hostess, her luminous eyes on Harold's square face.

"Depends on business."

"It's lovely up here. I love the snow. Just now I'm rather busy with Mr. Fenway's books — Mr. Blake Fenway's. Did you say whether you knew him, Mr. Hendrix?"

"I don't at all." Gamadge answered to his alias belatedly, and Harold grinned.

"He's wonderful." Her face glowed. "Wonderful. I used to help him in his New York library, but Aunt Alice thought there were so *many* of us." She laughed, and then grew grave. "Did you know about poor Mrs. Fenway, and Alden, and their awful trip?"

"Yes, I know all about them."

"All about *him?*"

"Yes, I know."

"Isn't it pitiful? We were so lucky to meet them, really, because Aunt Alice had to leave all her money behind her in occupied France. Aunt Alice is Mrs. Fenway's companion, and Mr. Fenway took me in too. He's simply an angel; I wish I thought I were being really useful. But we were able to do one thing for them all — we found Bill Craddock on the pier, and now he takes care of Alden."

"I understand that he's just the man for the job."

"He's splendid, you don't know how splendid," replied Hilda, "because he really isn't the right man at all."

"Isn't?"

Her whole face was suddenly downcast. "They'll never get anybody like Bill; but I should think it would kill him. I never was so surprised in my life as I was when I heard he was going to stay. He can't do anything physically hard yet, but he had such a nice offer from some friend of his to help run the indoors part of a dude ranch. I did so hope he'd take it. I thought of course he would! They wouldn't have paid him much, but it would have been so good for him."

"Perhaps he also wants to oblige Mr. Blake Fenway."

"Oh, there was no obligation for Bill; he just happened to meet us all, and he got us all here safely. You don't know what that boat was like. He wasn't nearly as well then as he is now, either. There were plenty of things he could have found to do here, and he had a lot of information he could have written up — about China, you know. Mr. Fenway was amazed when he said he'd stay on and look after Alden, and Aunt Alice was, too."

"Very exacting work, I should think."

"And for Bill, who's used to being so free and so much outdoors! He's looking very thin and pale."

"When did he make the decision?"

"Two years ago, I think."

"You've known Mr. Craddock a long time?"

"All my life," said Hilda. "His father and mother were friends of ours, and after mine died he used to keep turning up at my Swiss school — to keep me cheerful, you know."

"Your aunt wasn't on hand?"

"Oh no, she travelled about with Uncle. He had a business that took him everywhere; he represented a firm in America — the same one my father was in. Some kind of machinery. He and Aunt Alice lived outside Paris when they were at home; the nicest little house at a place called Bourg-la-Reine."

"I hope he comes and cheers you up at Fenbrook — Craddock does."

"He did at first; the Dobsons are so fond of Alden, and they used to keep him amused while Bill and I took walks. But he's too busy now, and we haven't the use of the cars, so Alden can't come." Her sad look changed, disappeared. "Of course his job comes first."

Mrs. Dobson brought in apple pie. When it was consumed they rose, and Gamadge admired the stately room. "They couldn't keep even their dishes in anything small or mean,

129

could they?" He ran his finger over the carving that framed a panel of one of the corner cupboards.

Hilda said laughing that one was a china closet and one wasn't. "But it all does look settled, doesn't it? Everything's so big!"

She led the way into the drawing room, and then, looking back at them, asked if they would like to see the library.

"Very much indeed."

"But I'm afraid it will be dreadfully cold. We keep that side closed up unless I'm working; then I have a gas stove."

"It may be cold for you." Gamadge looked at the thin cotton of the lavender dress. "Put on my coat."

Gamadge picked it up as they crossed the hall and hung it on her shoulders. She slipped her arms into it. "I'd like to keep it!"

Harold pushed back folding doors, and she switched on a light. It was a sombre old library, with latticed bookcases, framed engravings, ponderous mahogany, and furnishings of green rep. Gamadge said: "You can't have sent much down to New York; these shelves are pretty well tenanted still."

"I've shoved books along. The gaps don't show. The hard work is clearing out those cupboards underneath; the old papers and things were so dusty." She turned to a table heaped with papers and files. "I've been through every single one of them, because Mr. Fenway says a picture's gone out of a book. Did Mr. Mott tell you about it?"

"No. What?"

"Oh dear, the loveliest old book of views; at least I suppose it was lovely, Mr. Fenway says so. I remember what the set looked like — green-velvet bindings. A picture was missing when the books got to New York — torn out. A picture of old Fenbrook, the house they had at Peekskill. It can't be replaced. I was so sorry about it."

"Mightn't it have been torn out after the books got to New York?" Gamadge, smoking, leaned against the edge of the table; Harold was looking through a folder of old photographs.

"Oh, no!" She looked startled at the suggestion. "Mr. Fenway found that it was gone the day after the books came. And nobody would tear it out in New York!"

Gamadge smiled. "It's so much easier, isn't it, to suspect the featureless dead?"

"I didn't mean that. I only meant that we *know* it couldn't have been torn out at Number 24."

Gamadge stopped smiling as he looked at her drooping head. "Mr. Fenway doesn't blame you, I hope?"

"No, but I can't help wondering whether he thinks I handled it carelessly or something."

Harold made one of his isolated remarks: "You'd know if you yanked a picture out of a book."

"Yes, but I can't help worrying about it."

"Have you looked about the house?" asked Gamadge.

"Everywhere, all through the closets and the trunks and boxes in the attic. There are one or two locked closets, but they're just dress cupboards, I've seen them often when they were open; I think they're only locked because they come ajar. The family really did move out this autumn, you know, and packed things away. They never did before, Miss Fenway says. Have you met her?"

"No, never."

"She's so clever."

"When was this lost picture seen by anybody — do you know?"

"Twenty years ago, I think."

"Don't lose sleep over something that may have been lost before you were born," growled Harold.

"I'm afraid I never do lose sleep."

"Certainly must be quiet here at night."

"Oh, it is."

"Kind of lonesome?"

"No, I love it."

"Just you and the Dobsons," said Gamadge. "Are they near you at night?"

"Quite near; I have a southwest room on the next floor, and they're on the top floor in front."

"Quite near, as you say; too near for you to have any qualms at night?"

"I've never been frightened here but once, and that was only a week ago Thursday, such a cold, stormy night. It was silly of me, because imagine a burglar coming on a night like that!"

"Imagine." Gamadge smoked quietly, watching her.

"It wasn't a rat; Mr. Dobson says we have no rats. He thinks it was a squirrel; he says they sound just like people walking."

"What did this squirrel do?"

"I thought I heard somebody on the back stairs — they run past my room. And I thought I heard a bumping."

"Late at night?"

"Oh, yes. We were all sound asleep, it was after three o'clock. I thought that I'd first heard the noise in the attic. It's at the head of the back stairs. I wondered whether I ought to call Mr. Dobson, but the noises stopped, and it was so dreadfully cold, and I hated waking him. I did get up and look out into the hall, but everything was quiet. I was glad next morning that I didn't wake poor Mr. Dobson; the windows were all locked fast."

"It would have been rather a good night for a burglar, in one way, wouldn't it? His footsteps would have been covered by the snow."

"I think he would have been covered by the snow!"

"And he didn't come for the picture in the book of views, because it had reached New York by that time — hadn't it?"

"That very afternoon, and I never thought of it!"

"Why should you think of it?"

"Well." She looked puzzled. "It is a kind of a coincidence, in a way, isn't it? Two queer things happening."

"A picture goes, a squirrel comes?"

She laughed. "It's only because nothing queer has ever happened before at Fenbrook."

Harold asked: "Who's this of?" and held up a big studio photograph, much faded.

"That's Mrs. Fenway when she was young. Wasn't she lovely? But Aunt Alice says you can't tell *how* lovely, from a photograph. She had such wonderful color, and such blue eyes, and such glorious hair."

Gamadge looked at the picture of the tall girl in evening dress. "Beautiful woman," he said.

134

"She still is, *I* think. Mr. Hendrix, isn't it awful to think what can happen to people in only twenty-five years? She had everything; and now here she is, with no husband, and so badly hurt, and poor Alden to worry about, and only Aunt Alice to look after her."

"I suppose she could have had any number of people?"

"She wanted Aunt Alice because they're such old friends. She depends on her more and more. Even when the masseuse comes, she wants Aunt Alice there. Aunt Alice never leaves her at all, now."

"Doesn't come up to see you?"

"Oh, no. She can't. Only when they all come."

"Is this Mrs. Fenway's husband?" asked Harold, taking another photograph from the same folder.

"Yes, that's Mr. Cort Fenway. Wasn't he sweet?"

Gamadge agreed that there was sweetness in the long, smiling face.

"And that's Miss Fenway," said Hilda. "I think she's wonderful-looking, don't you?"

"A little disdainful?"

"People must irritate her because they're so dull. She's much kinder than she looks in that photograph, and so amusing. I wish I could talk to her."

Harold asked gloomily: "Is there some law?"

"I don't know enough," said Hilda, smiling at him. "I don't know anything."

A muffled hooting interrupted the conversation. Hilda gave Gamadge his coat, and he and Harold got hastily into their things. Gamadge said: "I won't try to thank you, Miss Grove, for your truly Christian hospitality."

"It's Mr. Fenway's." She smiled up at him. "I was only doing what he would have done; but I liked doing it! I've had such a nice time. I wish you could both come again."

As the taxi trundled out of the Fenway drive, Harold began to mutter. His mutterings at last became words:

"The picture gets torn out of the book the day the book gets to the Fenway house in New York. That night it's brought up and stowed in the Fenbrook garret. She's looked in the garret for it, but she didn't look where it was. Wonder what would have happened if she'd met Craddock coming down the back stairs. It was Craddock; Mrs. Grove couldn't make that hill from Rockliffe Station on a stormy night."

"She's fond of Craddock."

"Because she's known him all her life. What does she know about him really? He's knocked around, may have been up to anything. He'd

136

be able to get a key to the house; probably lots of them down at Number 24."

Gamadge was frowning in the dark. He said: "Don't *you* go bumping in the attic; not until I tell you to. And don't take a room at this inn that has no telephone in it. I may call you tonight, you know; I certainly will if I get results at that house, and in any case I'll ring you tomorrow. The deuce of it is that tomorrow's Monday, and I have to be in that office at nine. I have a lot of appointments. Don't know when I'll be able to take the books up to Fenway."

"That girl's kept up at Fenbrook to be out of the way of the blackmailers, it's a cinch she is. I don't know why the family stands for it — she's as lonely as the devil, whatever she says, and wasting her time."

"I'm afraid Miss Fenway doesn't want her at Number 24."

"How about Mr. Blake Fenway, so darned philanthropic as he is?"

"I'm afraid Mr. Blake Fenway thinks she's much happier at Fenbrook than she'd be at a business school or in an office."

"What was that stuff about a drawing of a head that looked like an old master?"

"Oh. Three heads — *Love Between Cruelty and Anger.*"

Harold said after a pause: "Don't let any-

137

thing happen to her, client or no client."

"My client doesn't want anything to happen." He turned his head and gave Harold a sardonic glance. "You don't mind staying up at the Oaktree now, do you?"

"At least she knows I'm there."

9

BREACH IN THE WALL

The dim and stuffy local crawled to a stop at sixteen minutes to nine. Gamadge hurried up the ramp and across the concourse to the nearest telephone. He called the Fenway number.

Mott Fenway answered. "Who is it? Who is it?" He sounded eager.

Gamadge replied in a kind of gobbling voice that astonished himself: "This is Charles Hendrix speaking, from the Vernon Club. Is this Mr. Mott Fenway?"

"Yes. Is this really Hendrix?"

"Himself."

"You sound as if you had a bad cold, Hendrix." The old gentleman chuckled.

"Touch of laryngitis. That bridge game, Fenway; could you join us tomorrow instead of Tuesday?"

"Tomorrow will suit me, old man."

"Er — as soon after nine as I can get there."

"You always were a punctual fellow."

The chuckling laugh was in Gamadge's ears

as he rang off. He redeemed his books from the checking office, and went for a cab.

He stopped the cab at his own street, parked his books in a friendly drugstore, and continued the journey uptown. He descended a block below the Fenways'. As he paid the driver, that individual remarked that there seemed to be some kind of trouble on the next corner.

"Trouble?" Gamadge looked up.

"People stopping there — at that big house."

Gamadge crossed the street and reached the small crowd almost at a run. An officer was on the nearer flight of the front steps, another beyond them; the radio car stood at the curb. The house door was open; it sent a stream of yellow light on staring faces. Blake Fenway and Craddock stood just outside the vestibule; Craddock's hand steadied the other, who half leaned against the side of the entrance doorway.

Gamadge shoved his way to the bottom step, and had his foot on it when a blue-clad arm got in his way. He felt as though he had been nudged by a safe.

Craddock's voice reached him. "Is that Mr. Gamadge?"

"Yes."

The young man's face was drawn into an

expression of forced calm, a lock of his black hair straggled down to his eyes. "Would you just come up? Get Mr. Fenway into the house?"

The policeman looked up at him, and at Gamadge; then he removed his arm, and Gamadge ran up the steps.

"If you'll just take him inside," said Craddock. "He mustn't stay here. Mr. Fenway, won't you go in? The other police and the newspapermen will be coming. You don't want to talk to them?"

The second radio policeman was now faced against the gate in front of the service door; behind him, within the railing, Gamadge saw a black shape against the snow. Sprawled there, it looked huge. Patches of gleaming wet were spreading across the hard icy crust of white.

"Accident. I want my cousin brought into the house; I can't leave him here," gasped Fenway.

"We can't move him, Mr. Fenway. I'll stay; I'll explain; I'll attend to it. Please go in. Mr. Gamadge, he needs a spot of brandy." Craddock let go of Fenway's arm. "I know how to talk to them," he said urgently.

Gamadge had Fenway by the elbow; he turned him gently, and got him into the house as a police car and another car came silently

141

around the corner from the avenue. He closed the door.

Caroline Fenway was coming down the stairs, trailing brown velvet. When she saw her father she ran the rest of the way, and put her arms around him. "Father, poor Father, I know. Phillips just told me." She looked at Gamadge. "Cousin Mott fell."

"I don't know why they won't let him be brought in," said Fenway. "I want him in his own room. Send for Thurley, Caroline."

"Phillips is telephoning. Mr. Gamadge, will you take my father into the back drawing room while I get him something — some brandy?" She added, as Gamadge again took Fenway by the elbow, "I don't know — were you passing by?" Her vague look steadied, became questioning.

"Yes. Craddock called me in and asked me to look after Mr. Fenway."

But the master of the house had pulled himself together. He walked stiffly and slowly at Gamadge's side through the dusk of the unlighted drawing room, under the faint sparkle of prisms on the chandelier, past the soft gleam of gold chairs and cabinets. The farther room was bright with lamps, and a fire burned in the grate; a room all gray and pale red, with a grand piano in the bow window and a glass-framed mirror above the gray marble man-

142

telpiece. The French clock said ten minutes past nine.

Fenway sat in a chair beside the fire. He got out a handkerchief, and pressed it to dry eyes. After a moment he looked at Gamadge. "I can't believe it. We were talking in the library, and the telephone rang. He answered it — not long before nine. He came back and said something about a bridge game tomorrow, and then he went upstairs. Went straight to his room on the top floor. Young Craddock was in his room next door, he heard him call out. He ran through; the window was open and no one there. He looked out — looked down."

Fenway paused. Gamadge said gently: "Frightful for you. But if he fell — if your cousin fell from the top story he must have died instantly."

"The officer said so. I explained — how my cousin always kept a window open while he was out of his room, and the door closed; not to make the rest of us cold, you know. Always so careful and so kind. My best friend. He went to close it, and those windows are low. I knew they were dangerous, I should have realized that he wasn't a young man. I wanted him brought into the house — why not, since it was plainly an accident? I wanted him on his own bed."

143

"They never do want a dead body moved, Mr. Fenway."

"It was Craddock that telephoned for the police. He didn't consult me; he called them before he told me what had happened. If I had only known, we could have brought my cousin into the house first."

"People would have crowded up, Mr. Fenway; you couldn't have handled it. And I'm quite sure that you'll have far less trouble and difficulty as it is; about getting it on the records and into the papers as an accident, you know; from the start."

Fenway sat with his handkerchief crumpled forgotten in his hand, his eyes wandering. "I respect the police, their job isn't an easy one; I understand their routine. But they so often leave the question open; suicide, you know. My cousin — it's quite absurd."

"If you'd moved him, Mr. Fenway, you might have had a lot of explaining to do. Craddock showed great presence of mind, I assure you."

"He went out there first; then he came and told me, and told Phillips. The radio car was very quick; they were here almost as soon as I had gone out myself."

Caroline appeared in the doorway that led to the back hall; Phillips came after her, a little decanter and glasses on a tray. He put the tray on a table beside Fenway. "I called Dr. Thurley, sir," he faltered, "and Officer Stoller's here."

"Oh — Stoller. Good. Stoller's the night man on our beat, Mr. Gamadge, a very good man. Knows us all. Knew my cousin. Phillips! You must call Bedlow."

"Yes, Mr. Fenway." Phillips's voice trembled.

"Bedlow will make arrangements for us. Where is Mr. Craddock?" Fenway began to struggle to his feet. "Why aren't they bringing Mott into the house, Caroline? I won't have him lying there."

Caroline had poured a little glassful of brandy. She had the glass in one hand; with the other she gently forced her father into his chair again. "Please let them do it as they must, Father. You can't interfere. Can he, Mr. Gamadge?" Her dark eyes were steady.

"Better leave them to manage it in their own way."

Fenway swallowed his brandy. "Somebody must tell your aunt, Caroline. Who's told your aunt?"

"Phillips. Mrs. Grove will look after her."

Gamadge, watching her, said: "Have a glass of that, Miss Fenway." As she made no move to pour herself one, he filled another of the little engraved bells on their delicate stems,

145

and handed it to her. "And sit down," he added. "You've had a bad shock too."

She gave him another steady look over her father's head. "So have you — haven't you?"

He returned the look quietly. "Of course."

"You're as white as a ghost; you'd better have some brandy yourself."

"Thanks."

They had their brandy, and Caroline sat beside her father. He put out his hand and clasped hers. "When I think that if Craddock hadn't been in his room Mott would have lain there — lain there —"

"Don't think of it. It's bad enough as it is, but poor Cousin Mott doesn't know."

"I'm very glad you happened to be passing, Mr. Gamadge. You understand these things — police procedure. If you'll stay and help us —"

"I'll be glad to do anything I can, Mr. Fenway."

"Somebody who knows police procedure, and happens to pass by. How lucky for us," murmured Caroline.

"I don't live so very far away, you know, and I have friends in this neighborhood."

They exchanged a look, unreadable on both sides. A large man appeared in the doorway; he was in uniform, and carried a nightstick; behind him loomed a still larger and taller

146

man, in plain clothes. He was light-haired, blue-eyed and square-faced. Another policeman in uniform, notebook in hand, brought up the rear.

"Stoller!" Fenway did rise this time.

"Yes, sir, and I was sorry I wasn't on the street when it happened." The first policeman put up a hand in salute. "It's a sad thing for you and Miss Fenway. Poor Mr. Mott, it was only last week I was talking to him in front of the house. I've been telling the Lieutenant what a nice man he was. This is Lieutenant Nordhall, sir; he wants to talk to you."

Lieutenant Nordhall said: "If it's convenient."

"Quite convenient. This is my daughter, and this is Mr. Gamadge, a friend who happened to be passing just after the accident occurred."

Nordhall, polite and grave, acknowledged these introductions. He then told Stoller that Stoller had better go back to his beat. Stoller withdrew, and the other uniformed man opened his notebook and screwed up his patent pencil.

"Officer Stoller," said Nordhall, "gave me some information, general information, useful. Mr. Craddock has been a lot of help; he's getting rid of the newspapermen for you. I've talked to your man Phillips, and I've seen the other servants. If I can have a few words with the family, that'll be all. Won't you take it easy, sir? Sit down?"

"My cousin's body, Lieutenant —"

"Well," Nordhall glanced at Caroline's calm face, and went on: "it's very badly injured, struck the railings. The people you wanted — Bedlow's — just came. Better let them take it, sir; bring it back tomorrow, next day."

"Yes. Very well." Fenway closed his eyes, and sat blindly down. Nordhall, looking polite sympathy, went on:

"Get all this over in no time. I've been over the scene of the tragedy, and I'm going to write it off as an accident."

"Anything else is out of the question, Lieutenant, of course."

"Looks so. Deceased went up to his room to close the window; high window, with a very low sill."

"Most dangerous, but he wouldn't have a guard."

"He put his arms up, the slots in the frame must have been about level with his chin; put his fingers in the slots, and his fingers slipped; for once he was careless. Pitched forward and out; the sill wouldn't reach his knees."

"If I had only realized that he was an old man! I should have insisted — but that's useless now."

"What I'm after — for the record — is the state of mind of the deceased prior to death. You understand."

"Of course. He was with me in the library, just across the hall; he was perfectly cheerful, I've never seen him depressed in my life. He had what is known as a happy disposition, Lieutenant. Some people called him happy-go-lucky, but that doesn't do him justice. He had had reverses in early life, but he was incapable of brooding; and for many years he has had no personal anxieties at all."

"Answered a telephone call, Mr. Craddock says."

"Oh — yes. Downstairs here."

"Telephone rang in the upstairs front room, Mr. Craddock answered. Somebody wanted to get up a bridge game."

"My cousin mentioned it when he came back to the library. He was looking forward to the game, tomorrow night I think it was to be."

"And then he went up to his room?"

"After a minute or so. We were going to play bridge ourselves — Craddock and I and my sister-in-law and her friend Mrs. Grove, who lives with us. My cousin Mott was anxious to finish some work he was doing on our income taxes. He did all that kind of thing for my daughter and me, and a great deal of it for my sister-in-law."

Nordhall looked at Caroline. "You saw the deceased after dinner, Miss Fenway?"

"Yes; we all had coffee upstairs, and then Cousin Mott came down to the library with my father. He was just as he always was. When they left the sitting room, I went into my own room and closed the door; I had some letters to write. The next thing I knew was when Phillips knocked at my door and said that there had been an accident, and that Cousin Mott had fallen out of his window. I came downstairs, and met my father and Mr. Gamadge coming into the house."

"Mrs. Fenway and Mrs. Grove and young Mr. Fenway —" Nordhall's tone was colorless — "stayed in the sitting room. Craddock left them there after he answered the telephone — or rather after he picked up the receiver and found that Mr. Mott Fenway was answering his own call. Craddock went up to his own room to wash his hands for the bridge game; he'd been getting them dusty mending some puzzle or other for Mr. Alden Fenway. He heard a shout or a cry, very much muffled, from Mr. Mott Fenway's room; must have been a loud cry the deceased gave, because Craddock heard it through two closed doors — the ones that lead from his room and Mr. Mott Fenway's room to that passage and bath.

He got through, and found an empty room and a wide-open window. Says he knew what had happened, and looked out. Then he rushed downstairs and out the front door. Found life extinct, ran in and telephoned the precinct. He did the only thing, Mr. Fenway; by the time he got outdoors again with you, people were gathering. You and he and that old butler of yours could never have managed alone; but let me say I understand you wanting to move the body. Of course you wouldn't want it lying out there practically in the street. Mr. Craddock did the right thing, though."

"I realize it now. I must tell him — thank him. I hope I didn't show anger at the time."

"He understands all that. He tells me that I can't expect evidence from Mr. Alden Fenway . . ."

"No. No."

"And I don't like to disturb the ladies upstairs; I think one of 'em's an invalid?"

"Not that; disabled."

"I don't like to disturb her; but if I can give out a statement to the press that the whole family says Mr. Mott Fenway was in a normal frame of mind —"

"I'll go up with you myself." Fenway rose. "And I should like to say that I am very grateful to you for the consideration you are showing us all."

"No other way for me to act. It's a straight case of accident, we could even check up with Craddock about that telephone call; that was a piece of luck for you, Mr. Fenway. There might have been some question — you know how some of these scandal sheets go on — about whether deceased had had bad news over the telephone."

"Bad news! He talked to me afterwards —"

"That's so. We won't," said Nordhall, with his first faint indication of a smile, "bother Mr. Hendrix."

"Hendrix?"

"Gentleman called him about the bridge game."

"Oh, yes; some friend of his at his little club."

"If we could go upstairs now?"

The uniformed man closed his notebook. Craddock appeared and came past him, his hair brushed back now from his forehead, and his face composed. He said: "All clear, Mr. Fenway."

"My dear boy, I don't know how to thank you. If it hadn't been for you, God only knows what I mightn't have done; you've saved us all from a lot of trouble and distress, I'm sure. Did you — did you see Bedlow?"

"Bedlow came himself. He'll be back in an hour to talk to you; the thing now is to get the street quieted down. I don't know where people come from." Craddock rubbed the back of his head.

"We're going upstairs now, to talk to Mrs. Fenway and Mrs. Grove. I don't want the boy upset; you'll come along?"

"Of course, sir." Craddock looked at Gamadge, and murmured: "Friend in need."

The others seemed to have forgotten all about him, and he could not imagine how to attach himself to them when they left the drawing room. He found himself alone with Caroline, wondering by what means he could possibly get himself upstairs. He did not even know how he could decently remain in the house.

Caroline solved the problem for him. She took a cigarette out of a box on a table, allowed him to light it for her, and said: "I want very much to talk to you."

"I'm at your service, Miss Fenway."

"Would you tell me why you came back to the house tonight? I won't repeat what you say."

They faced each other silently for a moment. Then Gamadge said: "I came by invitation."

"Whose?"

"Mr. Mott Fenway's."

10

CAROLINE

Caroline said: "Thank you for treating me like
an intelligent human being. I don't mean that
I'm more intelligent than the others, but they
haven't my reasons for thinking that you
didn't merely happen to pass by. Cousin Mott
told you this afternoon, didn't he, that we
thought Alden tore the picture out of the
book?"

"And that you thought Alden killed your
dog."

"He didn't agree with me about that. Let's
sit down, Mr. Gamadge; but first will you
close the door into the hall? You'll be able
to see straight through the front drawing
room; we shan't have eavesdroppers from that
direction."

Gamadge closed the door; it faced the entrance to the library, and as he came back
to the fire and sat down opposite Caroline he
wondered afresh why Mott Fenway had been
killed. He was sure they couldn't have been
overheard that afternoon, unless the Fenway

154

house were a trick house where privacy was an illusion and the walls had ears.

"I thought your cousin rather minimized the dangers of being listened in on," he said.

"He wasn't afraid; I am. I'm afraid of Alden. I was before, and now I have good reason to be. Don't you think so?"

She sat leaning back in her chair, velvet-clad knees crossed. One hand emerging from its long velvet sleeve lay open on her lap; when she raised her cigarette to her lips with the other, her ring sparkled.

Gamadge studied her gravely. At last he said: "Your nerve is good, Miss Fenway."

"Not as good as I pretend."

"You seriously think that your cousin Alden pushed Mr. Mott Fenway out of that window?"

"How can anybody know how a mind like his functions? They say it's a child's mind, but a vicious child isn't harmless. A child can do dreadful things, and physically Alden is a strong man. A child might strike a dog that irritated it; Alden killed the dog. A child might tear the page of a book; Alden tore it out and hid it cunningly. A child might give a person a push; Alden pushed Cousin Mott out of the window, and pretended he hadn't."

"Any evidence?"

"If I had evidence I shouldn't be troubling

you, and I shan't trouble you now unless you let me engage you professionally."

"That's out of the question. Mr. Mott Fenway is dead, and I can do nothing for him now; I'll be glad to do what I can for you. But I can't do much without evidence."

"If I had evidence I should take it to Aunt Belle; I should invite her to leave the house — with Alden."

"Invite *her* to leave?"

"She won't be separated from him. Her affection for him is morbid — she's never left him since he was born. She must have had plenty of chances to marry since Uncle Cort died, and he left her a small income, all he had. But I suppose no man wanted Alden in his household."

"You wouldn't take the evidence to your father?"

"Not if she agreed to put Alden in an institution for life. It would be no hardship for her to go elsewhere, Mr. Gamadge; the estate pays her enough to maintain them both in luxury; she could afford an army of servants to run a house. Why does she stay on here?"

"Your father ought to know what you think about Alden."

"I hope he never need hear a word of it. I really think it might kill him. It's a question of sentiment, and those questions can't be dealt with rationally. My father loved Uncle Cort, and Uncle Cort worshipped Aunt Belle, and Alden's their son. But I do think we shouldn't run such a fearful risk any longer. Who knows what grudge Alden may develop next? Perhaps the next one will be against my father."

"He had a grudge against Mr. Mott Fenway?"

"That's the worst of it — he never showed anything of the kind. But he's never seemed the pathetic being to me that others think him; I meet him wandering in the hallways and I turn cold. It's ridiculous to have no attendant for him but a nervous half-invalid like Bill Craddock, who knows nothing about mental disease; and I'm not sure that Bill wouldn't conceal even this for Alden's sake. If Alden did kill my dog, Bill Craddock must have been the one who concealed the fact."

"If he killed Mr. Mott Fenway, his mother and Mrs. Grove must be lying to save him."

"They'll never admit he was out of the sitting room."

"Mrs. Grove wouldn't?"

"She's utterly dependent on Aunt Belle, and she has the niece to think of. I don't like to think that Bill Craddock would lie about such a dangerous thing, but he's quite penniless at present except for his salary, and not able to earn money in the usual ways; and he wants to get married."

"To Miss Grove? Your cousin Mott Fenway said something."

"Hilda Grove is penniless too, and Father doesn't want her to plunge into marriage with a man in Bill's circumstances, a man she doesn't even seem to be particularly in love with." Caroline smiled a little. "Poor father couldn't make a blighted romance out of it. He thinks she's a rare creature, he wants to give her a beautiful life; he hopes that I shall be able to introduce her to eligibles. She's a very nice girl indeed, but I don't think it will be easy to marry her off. It never would have been easy — there are so many nice girls in the world! And now most of the nice young men are otherwise engaged. Father is romantic about women, you know; he would have liked to be romantic about me."

"He wants to shelter them?"

"When they're like Hilda. There must be something special about her, though, that escapes me. At present she seems quite happy at Fenbrook, and I certainly don't grudge her that bleak shelter and the Dobsons."

"She's not in love with Mr. Craddock?"

Caroline smiled faintly again. "She 'doesn't know'. She's known him always, and Father thinks she ought to meet other young men.

But she's young, her problems will solve themselves."

"Yours are more immediate."

"They are indeed. I hoped *you'd* try to find evidence for me, Mr. Gamadge — they say you're so good at that."

"Evidence that Alden Fenway killed Mott Fenway? If there is evidence, the police have it now."

"The police?" She sat up, amazed. "They're convinced that it was an accident!"

"They accept the accident theory provisionally, but they take nothing for granted."

"Lieutenant Nordhall was *pretending?*"

"Being considerate. I dare say he'll find nothing, but he'll miss nothing. Your cousin's body will be examined, you know; for bruises."

"Bruises? Cousin Mott fell from the top of the house down on an iron railing!"

"There might be ante-mortem bruises on the back of the head or on the shoulders."

She frowned. "There won't be!"

"No; a slight push would have been enough, and a slight push doesn't leave a bruise. But they'll look. I'll be glad to go over the scene with you, however, and I should very much like to see your aunt and Mrs. Grove. If they think as you do, they must be in a frightful state."

"Father will have told them that you're here; I could take you in. But I'm not at all sure that you'll learn anything from them; they're used to hiding what they feel!"

"Used to it?"

"That brings me to the view of old Fenbrook, Mr. Gamadge. I'm absolutely convinced that Alden tore it out and has hidden it, and that there's evidence on it that he did tear it out. And I'm convinced that he's told Aunt Belle something about it, and that she's told Mrs. Grove. Ever since the day the books came into the house they've been like — I can only compare them to clockwork figures; wound up and tense. They sit there doing their everlasting needle point, never even talking to each other, and I should think they'd go mad; and Aunt Belle keeps looking at Alden in a kind of desperation. And they're looking for the picture — at least Mrs. Grove is, or perhaps Bill Craddock. I've heard people wandering about downstairs, but I've never done anything about it. I was afraid to look myself, because I was afraid it might be Alden and that I should meet him in the dark; and if it had been one of the others, and I called Father and made a fuss, they'd simply say they were looking for a book or something. What *could* I do?"

"Not much."

"It's easy to get about this house without being seen; I could take you up by the back stairs now and we shouldn't be seen at all; the servants will be in their basement sitting room unless they're rung for."

"Let's go by all means." Gamadge rose and dropped his cigarette into the fire. "After all, there may be evidence on the top floor that Nordhall hadn't the special knowledge to interpret."

"And you may get some idea where to look for the picture." Caroline had risen also. "Perhaps we ought to go over the whole house?"

"We can't do much tonight; but if you like I'll come back tomorrow. I can bring your father that first edition, you know; but I won't shock Phillips by asking to see him or anybody."

"Phillips will have orders to tell me when you come."

"The trouble is, I don't know quite when I *can* come. I have to see people tomorrow, and they can't be put off; some of them come a long way."

"I'll wait in all afternoon." She paused, and looked at him gravely. "This matter can't seem very important to you, Mr. Gamadge, I realize that; compared, I mean, with the kind of thing you must be fighting now."

"Not important? It's a manifestation of the powers of evil."

"I shouldn't give it such an imposing name as that. After all, it was the work of a mental deficient."

"If your assumptions are correct we may figuratively call it the work of one possessed of an evil spirit; and that work is being condoned by persons who owe your father frankness, and who are all — even Mrs. Fenway — actuated by self-interest. If," he repeated, "your assumptions are correct."

"At any rate, they're all making the rest of us run a fearful risk. Mr. Gamadge — if you don't find the picture in a day or so I *will* speak to Father."

"Good."

"Shall we go straight up to the top floor, then?"

"If you'll first describe the basement story. I think I know this one pretty well."

"When you come in from the yard there's a lobby — that's where my dog slept."

"Did he bark at members of the household?"

"Well, I must admit that he was apt to greet them joyfully. He was a wonderful dog, Mr. Gamadge; a Dalmatian."

"I'm sorry you lost him."

"It seems — almost like a murder to me.

It's very hard for me to make allowances for Alden. Well, there's the lobby, with the billiard room opening off one side of it and the laundry off the other. In front is a long passage that runs right through the house, and all the other rooms are on the east side of it; the kitchens and pantries, a bathroom, the servants' sitting room and Phillips' bedroom and bath."

"Has he a telephone?"

"There's one in the hall outside his door." She added: "I don't somehow think that Alden would hide the picture downstairs, and he would have been seen if he'd hidden it out of doors in the garden."

"We mustn't make too many assumptions, you know."

"Of course not."

Gamadge opened the hall door for her; to his surprise she went straight across to the door next that of the library.

"Isn't that a pantry?" he asked.

"Oh, no."

She opened the door, and Gamadge saw a short passage ending in a narrow, carpeted stairway. He stood staring.

"There's a little hall like this on every floor," explained Caroline, "shut off from the main part of the house. These stairs come out in the basement lobby." She looked at him.

"What's the matter, Mr. Gamadge? You look stunned."

Gamadge was momentarily stunned; he now knew why Mott Fenway had lost his life. "I'm admiring my own stupidity," he said. "I thought the back stairs were behind that glassed door at the end of the hall."

"No, that's a conservatory, complete with rubber plants and palms. There are horrid little ferns there, too, which Phillips nurses and puts into a legendary silver dish on the dinner table. Here's a telephone, as you see, and the door on the right leads to the pantry. The one on the left belongs to the library, of course."

"Of course." Gamadge could almost see an eavesdropper creeping down the back stairs, listening to the conversation in the library, taking in (perhaps with some amusement) his own fatuous arrangements for keeping the conversation private. He followed Caroline up two steep flights to the top floor; on this landing a ladder rose to a blacked-out skylight.

Caroline opened the door to the main hall, glanced right and left, and beckoned. He again followed.

"You see there's a glassed door at the end of this corridor, too," she said, "and there's one on the second floor. They belong to big bathrooms. The servants' quarters and the trunk rooms and store closets are opposite and to our right. This room on our left — it's above mine — is the only guest room left to us, and we didn't even have *it* until Hilda Grove moved to Fenbrook!"

"It really has been something of an invasion."

"It really has! The two front rooms are Cousin Mott's and Bill Craddock's; his door is down that cross passage. Cousin Mott and Bill shared a communicating bath and a long clothes cupboard."

Gamadge walked past the guest room and through the open doorway of a large, comfortable, shabby bachelor's apartment. It had a threadbare Turkey carpet, ancient and huge mahogany furniture, ancient and faded group photographs in frames, a student lamp converted to electricity. The west and north windows, thickly curtained with dark madras, were now closed.

Caroline had remained on the threshold. She said: "He wouldn't let us buy him new things or even give him a carpet; these were all his own, and most of them were with him when he was in college. He failed in business ever so long ago, and afterwards came and lived with us. Why not? Everybody can't make money. We loved having him, and he did all kinds of things for Father. He stayed here in the summers while we were away, so we never had to close up the house; he hated travelling and country resorts. He always took me to the circus when I was little, and to funny plays afterwards. He was so nice."

"And you were so nice." Gamadge went to the tall window above the sitting-room bay, bent, and touched the sill. When he straightened he showed Caroline the powdery flakes on his fingers.

"I told you Nordhall wouldn't overlook anything," he said. "The professional as against the amateur — me."

He put his fingers into the two brass slots in the window frame; it rose easily as high as his chin. He stood looking out at the dark side wall of the opposite house, and then down at the street. A man in a cap was clearing stained and trampled snow out of the space within the railing; somebody — Nordhall, perhaps — was getting into an official car. It drove off, and only a patrolman remained to deal with the thinning crowd.

Gamadge closed the window and turned. "You could have sent me out of that with a turn of the wrist," he said, "and nobody the wiser, not even the policeman below. The street's too dark."

"We'll have a fine new guest room," said Caroline in a dry voice, "and Father will have

166

guardrails put on all these windows."

Gamadge walked through a long bathroom, through a passage lined with closet doors, and into Craddock's not very cheerful retreat. It was rather untidy, with a portable typewriter on a chair and a kit bag under a table. Battered toilet articles were strewn on the plain cover of an outmoded bureau.

Caroline had come the other way, along the transverse hall. She stood at the door. "This was Father's room when he was a boy," she said, "and Uncle Cort had the other. It's horrid now. Our footman had it before he was drafted."

"Mr. Craddock is a bird of passage." Gamadge looked at the kit bag. "You can see that he's lived in his luggage for years."

"Alden could have run into the guest room, or even down the back stairs, before Bill got through to Cousin Mott's room."

"Yes. Plenty of lines of retreat."

"Alden's room downstairs has a door into the hall. He could have crossed to the back stairs in two seconds."

"We'll go down."

They went along the hall and descended the wide main stairway; halfway down Caroline leaned over the balustrade. "I'm afraid they've gone to bed; it's dark."

"We might see how much of the hall would

have been in their line of vision."

"Practically none, if they were where I left them — beside the fire. But it won't make any difference — they'll never admit that Alden was out of the room."

They went into the sitting room, and Caroline turned on a lamp. Gamadge asked, looking at the closed door in the east wall: "Shall we disturb them?"

"Not if we speak quietly; the doors are soundproof. I ought to know — that was my mother's suite; Aunt Belle has the front room now, and then there's a bath, and Mrs. Grove has the little dressing room. Next her is Alden's, with a door into the hall as I told you."

"Where are you, and where is your father?"

"I'm just outside here, the first door on the right as you go out; I have my own bath. Father's suite is beyond the back passage; two rooms and a bath, the whole southwest corner of the house."

Gamadge turned to look at the half-open door of her room; then he walked to the embrasure of the bay. "The window's closed, I see. Those ladies don't seem to have heard the commotion after your cousin fell."

"They needn't have heard it; everything's thick and solid and noiseproof in this house."

The round table stood where it had stood

that afternoon, and the wastebasket just below it was half full of colored snippings from the day's needle work; but on top of the soft mass lay a crumpled paper ball. He had expected to see it there, his client had trusted him to come and find it. In his momentary triumph Mott Fenway's death and Caroline's quest faded from his mind.

11

SECOND ARROW

"What in the world, Mr. Gamadge," asked Caroline, "are you digging out of the waste-basket?"

Gamadge straightened, glanced at the paper ball, and dropped it into his pocket. "A memorandum I threw away this afternoon by accident. Lucky to find it again."

"If our footman hadn't gone to the wars you wouldn't have found it; the basket would have been emptied before dinner."

A well-dressed man with an air of cool authority came out of Mrs. Fenway's bedroom. He was carrying a black bag. "Well, Caroline!" He stopped to look at her, professionally enough, but also with a manner at once friendly and paternal. "Do *you* want some of the sedatives I stuffed into my bag, or can you manage without them?"

"I can manage, Doctor."

"I thought you could." He put the bag on the table, and looked at Gamadge.

"This is Mr. Gamadge, Dr. Thurley."

Gamadge nodded in response to Thurley's nod. He liked the look of the Fenways' family doctor; a graying, ruddy, muscular man.

"Glad to meet you, Mr. Gamadge," said Thurley. "Craddock tells me that if you hadn't happened along Blake Fenway would probably still be putting ideas into the heads of the press. I've put my official seal on the accident theory; Mott Fenway would have lived a hundred years, if he'd been able to manage it, and enjoyed every day of them. Wish there were more like him; wish some of the rest of us understood leisure. I shall miss him. Caroline, your father's talking funeral arrangements with old Bedlow in the library; they'll be at it half the night if you don't go down and interfere. My orders, and he's to take those pills I gave him. If he doesn't he'll lie awake."

"I'll go, Doctor." She looked at Gamadge, who answered the look by saying that he would get himself out of the house.

"Then — tomorrow?"

"Sometime in the afternoon."

"Good night."

"Good night, Miss Fenway."

When she had gone he addressed Thurley, who was rearranging the contents of his bag. "I thought you might want a prescription filled, or something; I know what deliveries

171

are now, especially at night."

"Very thoughtful of you, but I had the presence of mind, as I told Caroline just now, to throw some old reliables into my bag before I rushed up here. I've dosed Belle Fenway, or at least I've left a dose to be taken. Mrs. Grove will get it down her if she's restless."

Gamadge walked across the room to the lamp, got the paper ball out of his pocket, and smoothed it out. It was another section of timetable, and there was another arrow in the margin; but this arrow pointed nowhere; away from Rockliffe Station into space.

He put the crumpled leaf in his pocket again. Thurley was talking:

"Shocking tragedy, and cruel hard on Blake Fenway. There's bound to be a little publicity; dear old Mott was obscure personally, but he was a Fenway. The police are behaving very well; I saw Nordhall, competent man. He'll have them make a routine examination of the body, and then he'll give out a definite statement to the newspapers. Blake doesn't understand these things, but he's always willing to do what's proper. The perfect citizen. Of course he's badly shaken up; he feels responsible on account of those devilish windows. Do you know Belle Fenway?"

"I met her this afternoon."

"Heroic creature, can face anything. I'll

have her on her feet in less than a year, I hope, but it will take time — time and surgery. She got no care on the trip home in 1940, impossible conditions. I'm only glad the experience didn't drive young Alden out of the wits they built up for him in Europe. They did wonders for him, I'll say that for the Frenchmen. I saw him regularly from the time he was born until he was four, and I never thought he could be maintained at a four-year level. Viborg was optimistic, if you can call it optimism, thought the boy would develop to five-year-old mentality. They did better in Fagon's clinic. Have you seen Alden Fenway?"

"Yes."

"Fagon said he could be kept at the seven-year level unless there should be disease of the brain and quick deterioration. The boy does very well; takes complete care of himself. Craddock's the very man for him, and I'm only afraid they won't be able to keep him frozen on the job."

"What chances are there for further improvement in young Fenway? Or further development, let us say? Do the mental specialists commit themselves?"

"He's had none since they came back to this country; Belle won't face it. It seems that he's always upset by tests, and it takes him a long

time to get used to a new man. Viborg's retired, and of course Alden wouldn't remember
him in any case. The boy was very shy with
me at first, but now we're great pals."

Gamadge scribbled *Work in Progress* on an
envelope, crumpled it, and crossed the room
to toss it into the wastebasket. Then he scribbled on another, which he placed carefully in
his wallet.

"Pretty lavish with good letter paper, aren't
you, young man?" Thurley snapped his bag.

"Damned wasteful. I never can remember
to conserve it. How is Alden taking tonight's
tragedy, Doctor?"

Thurley, making for the door, stopped halfway. "Doesn't know a thing about it. He'll
inquire after Mott once or twice, and then
forget him. Well, I'll be getting along. See
you again, I hope, in more cheerful circumstances." He hurried out, and down the stairs.
Gamadge thought that the doctor was capable
of making almost any circumstances cheerful.

They have to be like that, he thought; grow
an extra skin. They'd never survive it all if
they didn't — be of no use to anybody.

He turned out the light and went into the
hall; silence here, darkness except for one
shaded bulb that did not reach the farther
shadows. Psyche's lamp was unlit, herself a
wraith just visible in her little arched shrine.

174

As he reached the landing in front of her the ghost of a sound made him look over his shoulder; Alden Fenway's bedroom door opened, and the young man came out. He was in his shirt sleeves, with his collar unfastened and a comb in his hand; evidently on his way to the bathroom.

He stopped to look down at Gamadge. He seemed to tower in the dusky light, a little terrifying; like a giant walking doll with a fixed smile, whose mechanism was a mystery.

He asked: "Do you live here now?"

"Very sensible question; no."

"Then come again soon."

"Thanks, I will."

Gamadge went on down the stairs, wondering what it would feel like if one of those big hands spread itself between his shoulder blades.

Rummaging in the closet beneath the stairs, he found his hat and coat. He let himself out into the vestibule, and came face to face with Craddock.

"Mr. Gamadge — you're going?"

"Well, yes; at last."

"It's only half past ten."

"I rather thought it must be the day after tomorrow."

"Tired? I am myself. But if you'd just spare me a few minutes . . ."

Craddock looked more than tired; fatigue and strain had given him the wild expression of a man in physical misery. Gamadge said: "As many minutes as you like."

"I thought — don't want to disturb them in there. If you'd come down to the billiard room?"

Gamadge followed him down to the street, along to the gate in the railing, through it to the service door. Craddock unlocked this, and locked it behind him when they had entered a paved yard. Trees and shrubbery were on their right, and beyond opened the snowy expanse that would be grass some day. Craddock unlocked the kitchen door, and they went into a short entrance hall. There was a doorway to left and right; Craddock led the way through the right-hand one and turned a switch.

The big room was pretty well occupied by a billiard table, a ping-pong table, two bridge tables and several chairs. Divans ran the length of the south and west walls, and there was a fireplace opposite the long west window.

Craddock said: "It's cold down here; I'll light the fire."

"Not for me; keep my coat on."

"Well — all right."

They sat on the divan nearest the doorway, their coats on and their hats pushed forward

176

by the leather cushions against which they leaned; two exhausted-looking men. "Nice place," said Gamadge. "Must be a great place in good weather, cool and pleasant with the garden outside."

"Yes. Mott Fenway liked it down here. I can see him knocking the balls around of an evening, played a good game. Played everything well. Took on any of us at ping-pong, even. I liked him, even if he didn't think much of us."

"Us?"

"The other crowd; Mr. Fenway's."

"Oh."

"I didn't blame him entirely, we do fill the house up. But it was tough on Mrs. Fenway. He thought a lot of *you;* he talked about you yesterday, after we all heard you were coming, and again today at lunch. Mr. Gamadge — did he ask you to come back here tonight?"

Gamadge was lighting a cigarette. "What makes you think so?"

Craddock pulled a standing ash receiver towards them with his foot. He said: "You didn't happen along by accident; and he had a chance to talk to you alone this afternoon, when he took you downstairs."

"So did Mr. Blake Fenway have a chance to talk to me alone."

"He's out of it."

"Why should Mr. Mott Fenway ask me to come back here tonight?"

Craddock got out his own cigarettes. He said, choosing one, "I don't know where I stand. We'll have to settle that before I say anything, if it can be settled. Mrs. Grove knew my people, and she got me this job at a time when I couldn't have held down another to save my life; but Mrs. Fenway's paying me, Alden's my patient — you might call him that, I suppose — and I'm under Blake Fenway's roof. And Blake Fenway treats me like a king."

"Am I to tell you whom you're to be loyal to?" Gamadge turned his head to look at the young man. Craddock, however, did not look at him. He went on:

"I shouldn't say a word to you or anybody if I hadn't a personal motive for talking — Hilda Grove. I haven't an atom of proof to back anything I say. I thought you might be willing to advise me, and then forget about it. I wouldn't suggest this if I had evidence, but as I remarked before, there's none."

"You'll have to trust my discretion."

Craddock looked at Gamadge, his black eyes burning as if there might indeed be fever in his blood. He said: "At least I'm pretty sure you're not the kind of reforming busybody that finally gets had up for slander."

"No," replied Gamadge, smiling; "I'm not that."

"I ought to tell you frankly that I'm not actuated by any higher motive myself than personal affection. Hilda's parents were killed in a plane crash; Mrs. Grove showed up and put her in that Swiss school, and then sheered off again. I made it my business to look in on young Hilda whenever I was within a thousand miles, more or less, of Geneva. I knew her when she was a baby; she's one still, in some ways — doesn't question motives, doesn't look for slights, has no vanity. I wish you'd met her; you'd get some idea of how I feel."

"I'll try to exercise my imagination."

"The point is that she can't fight her own battles, and that she has nobody to look after her but Mrs. Grove — a dry stick if ever I saw one. I stayed on this job instead of going west because I thought she ought to have one friend in the offing. Blake Fenway is a king, but he lets Caroline keep Hilda marooned up there at Fenbrook with two rather stupid old servants. Mrs. Fenway's no use, has no authority and can't walk. Now I get the idea that there's something definitely wrong about Mrs. Grove. I never liked her much, but I thought she was a high-principled kind of type. Lately I'm not sure about it."

"How lately?"

"Since that nuisance of a book got into the house; that book of views. It brought things to a head, somehow, but I think the trouble goes back farther than that, much farther. I know Mott Fenway thought Alden had torn the picture out; I heard him asking the poor guy questions about it. Alden didn't know what it was all about; he's a nice fellow, would have been a great guy if he'd ever had a chance. I'm fond of him; he has a great disposition, he's never sulky or troublesome. Perhaps he did tear the picture out; but I think Mott Fenway had stumbled on something else — overheard the two women talking, or found some letter. He wanted to get rid of the whole bunch of us, and I don't think he would have stuck at much to do Caroline Fenway a favor. She hates the sight of us all." Craddock leaned forward, his elbows on his knees. "My idea is that Mrs. Grove has something on Mrs. Fenway — something about Alden. They've been in Europe for years, probably met often. It's possible that Alden may have been tagged by the psychiatrists over there — got into trouble of some kind, and Mrs. Grove knows it and is cashing in."

"What kind of trouble?"

"Something that wouldn't matter a damn if he had his wits. He oughtn't to be allowed out alone, you know; as likely as not to stop traffic forgetting to cross the street with the lights. Mrs. Fenway may have been careless — he's so decently behaved that it's hard to remember he isn't all there. And people like Alden aren't allowed even one mistake, you know; one break, and that's the finish. And Mrs. Fenway has this idea that he's better off among normal surroundings; she thinks he'd get stupid and miserable away from her. She may be right."

"What gave you the idea that Mrs. Grove is cashing in?"

"Anybody with eyes in his head can see that there's trouble between her and Mrs. Fenway. Mrs. Fenway is under a terrific strain, and the other woman doesn't leave her for a minute. The room's full of dynamite. I'd say it had something to do with the telephone. Mrs. Grove sits looking at it, and Mrs. Fenway never touches it. It was an inch away from her hand tonight, but I had to come over and take that message for Mott Fenway. By the way, do you know that nobody's bothered to call Hilda and tell her Mott's dead? She was fond of him. I'd have called her myself, but I solemnly swore to Blake Fenway that I wouldn't."

"Wouldn't telephone to Miss Grove?"

"Or write, or see her alone. He thinks she was sliding into a relationship with me that

181

wasn't fair to her. He thinks I was getting a monopoly. He wants her to meet other men before she makes up her mind; I don't blame him, I'm no catch; couldn't support a canary bird. But how is she to meet other men, or anybody, up there at Fenbrook?"

"These war conditions hold things up."

"I don't think war conditions have much to do with it. Miss Fenway wants the house cleared, and this business about Hilda is a kind of passive resistance she's working."

"Why should the telephone come into the blackmailing scheme, if there is one?"

"I'm just making up a story to account for the state of things upstairs, you understand; I thought somebody might be coming here from Europe who could blow the information about Alden, and that they're expecting the call."

"Why shouldn't they take it, then?"

"Mrs. Fenway doesn't dare, and Mrs. Grove wants an independent witness to get the name of the party first, so Mrs. Fenway will know it's all on the level and come across with a final payment or something. I think she's staying on here because the other woman is getting all her money. Salting it away."

"This is hindsight, Mr. Craddock."

"It's not; I'm telling you what I've observed myself since a week ago Thursday."

"You wouldn't have said a word about it if Mott Fenway hadn't been killed this evening."

"All right then." Craddock sat up, threw away his cigarette, and faced Gamadge. "That means you agree with me about that accident. I think he asked you to come back here and advise him about the Alden Fenway situation, or Mrs. Grove's blackmail game. I think he was shoved out of that window to prevent his spilling it to you. I was glad to see you tonight, but I don't believe in miracles — after you'd gone into the house my brain began working. There weren't any accidents; your coming along when you did wasn't one, Mott Fenway's death five minutes earlier wasn't one. And the next crime the Grove woman commits may involve Hilda, but by that time I'll be drafted to God knows where."

Gamadge extinguished his cigarette; when he spoke it was amiably, but without enthusiasm:

"You're in a difficult situation, created however by yourself from a mass of conjecture. Let's see whether your ingenuity can cope with a couple of plain questions. What did Mott Fenway expect me to do for him?"

"How can I tell, when I don't know what he'd found out? He may have thought you could advise him how to tackle Mrs. Grove and get rid of her without publicity. Scare her off."

"And what am I to do for you?"

"The same thing, if —" Craddock's face was suddenly the face of a distraught and embarrassed young man — "if you only will. I thought if you were willing to advise him you'd be willing to advise me; since he's dead."

"But according to you, murder's been committed now. Are you prepared to turn a murderess loose on the community with a warning?"

"There's no evidence against her. Mrs. Fenway won't say that she left the sitting room; she's afraid to. I heard her tell Nordhall that all three of them were there all evening."

"But suppose there should be evidence?"

"Then I say tell the police. It won't kill Hilda — she and Mrs. Grove aren't blood relations. I say get rid of that woman somehow. Worse things can happen than murder trials."

"Worse things for Miss Grove?"

"Yes. If you'll only help me get her out of the clutches of the woman!"

"I must say I'd like a few facts to bolster up these startling theories of yours. You were in the sitting room when Nordhall questioned the ladies. How did they behave?"

"Mrs. Fenway was terrified; kept looking

at Mrs. Grove, and when she talked her teeth were chattering. Mrs. Grove put on her usual act; but it wasn't as good as usual. I thought she looked ready to faint herself."

"She's a small woman, not in her first youth; but I suppose it wouldn't take much of a push to send the old gentleman out of the window. But you were in the next room all the time."

"She didn't know that; I don't go up to my own room to wash up if I'm on the second story; I use the bathroom at the end of that hall. I went up tonight because my nails needed a spot of manicuring if I was to play bridge. She was sitting to the left of the fireplace in the sitting room; wouldn't have seen where I went or what I did. She'd be safe until she got right up behind Mott Fenway, and then it was only a matter of seconds for her to shove him out and dash for the back stairs."

"Risky."

"Better than having *you* in the house, listening to what he had to say. But she was safe enough. I heard that yell, and it took me a few seconds to locate it; you know the way you stand gaping. Then I ran through to our bathroom, got the near door open, got his door open, and of course never looked at anything afterwards but the open window — and his body lying down there below. When I first leaned out it was just falling away from the rail." Craddock put a hand up to his forehead, pushing his hat to the back of his head. "Can't forget it. I've seen worse, but I can't forget it."

Gamadge rose to his feet, turned up his collar, and pulled on his thick gloves. He said: "I saw him on the snow. I won't forget it either."

Craddock looked up at him. "*Can* you do anything?"

"I'll think it over. I'm coming in tomorrow — see you then."

"Coming back?" Craddock, still seated, gazed at him frowning.

"Yes. I'm bringing a first edition to Mr. Blake Fenway."

"First . . . look here! That's no kind of excuse. You won't get past Phillips with it."

"Perhaps someone will invite me in — as you did tonight." Gamadge faintly smiled.

186

12

GASLESS VEHICLE

Gamadge took a cab to the drugstore where he had left the books, got his parcel, and drove home. He left all but the book of views in his office; the flat green quarto he took upstairs with him to the library.

His wife and Arline Prady were playing backgammon. Clara sprang up and rushed to him as usual; Arline looked disappointed.

"Where's Harold?" she asked.

"In the suburbs."

"Oh. Then I'll be going."

This did not mean that Arline only liked to be at the Gamadges' when Harold was there; she always liked to be at the Gamadges', but she had been brought up to think that no man can bear the sight of an extra woman.

"You mustn't go," said Gamadge. "I have a job for you."

Arline's face lighted. "Did you say a *job?*"

"With full operative's pay and expenses. But I can't tell you about it till I've had something to eat. I'm rather hungry."

Clara dashed for the little elevator; Arline followed. Gamadge mixed himself a highball, and then brought the telephone in and set it down beside the chesterfield. He reclined against pillows and called the Oaktree Inn.

After a long wait Harold's voice addressed him: "You didn't get bopped?"

"No. Somebody else had the accident; the party who expected me."

There was a pause. Then Harold said: "You don't tell me so."

"For further details see your morning paper."

"I don't think you have to worry about anybody up here but central. There's nobody on the switchboard downstairs, the place is dead. The night clerk sends up calls, but he'll be asleep again by this time."

"No harm in exercising caution."

"Did you get into the place?"

"Twice; once by the front door, once by the door in the wall. I've been invited back tomorrow by several persons."

"Then you'll have a chance to get another message."

"I got it. It was waiting for me in the same place. Weekday section of the timetable, and an arrow; but the arrow points the other way."

Harold pondered this. "*Away* from the place?"

"Away from the place."

After another pause Harold said: "I think I get it."

"Whether we're right or not, we'll have to act on the suggestion."

"But how can we work it?"

"I'll think that over and call you in the morning. Arline's here; I may send her up."

"Glad to have company. There's one other resident guest — an old guy that eats dinner in spats and a skull cap."

Gamadge rang off, and sat up to face a small table which Arline was setting out with biscuits, cheese, and part of a cold chicken. He wondered why she and Harold were not married; perhaps they were, though, and shy about announcing it. Arline was Harold's slave, and Harold guarded his private life jealously.

Clara arrived with a dish of fruit and a pot of instantaneous coffee. Gamadge fell to. After a minute he said: "I begin to feel better. The Fenway house is not a house of peace and light; evil dwells therein, formless as yet but taking shape. Taking shape. I can't tell you about it tonight, it's too late and I'm too confoundedly tired; but you must have a bare outline. Arline, will you be good enough to open that flat green book I put on the table? I shouldn't like to spill coffee on it."

Arline opened the book of views.

"And turn to a plate with the title: *Mansion and Grounds of J. Delabar King, Esq.*"

"Here it is," said Arline. "A very pretty house."

"Place a marker at the page, and then find *The Classic Home of Colonel Ash.*"

"I have it."

"Clara, will you get the reading glass from my desk?"

Clara obeyed.

"The book," continued Gamadge somewhat chokingly, since he had had rather a large mouthful of chicken, "once contained a view of Fenbrook, the ancestral home of the Fenways. That home has vanished, and there is a new Fenbrook at Rockliffe-on-Hudson."

"Here's the piece about it," said Arline, "but the picture's torn out."

"The picture of old Fenbrook; it has been removed within the last twenty years — I myself think within the last two weeks — by some party unknown. The book is a book that Mr. Cort Fenway, twenty years deceased, loved to pore upon. When I pored upon it this afternoon in the Fenway Library I thought I saw evidence that Mr. Cort Fenway had used it as a writing block. There are incised marks on the plates Arline found for me, and on their tissue guards; I should say that the marks had

190

come through the tissue guards upon the plates. Will both of you see what you can make of them with the reading-glass?"

Arline said: "This Delabar King picture had a letter written on top of it. Clara, can you make out the signature?"

"There's a capital C, and a small v — or is it half a w? — and the tail of a — let's see — a y."

"But none of the letter part is legible?" asked Gamadge.

They assured him that it was not, and Clara brought him a paper on which she had copied what could be read of the signature. He saw *C   w y,* and supplied dots. The result was *C . . . . w. y.*

"There you are," he said. "*Cort Fenway.* Now try the other plate."

Clara and Arline labored, and at last Clara brought Gamadge the following reconstruction: *. y d . . . . st, so . nx . o . s,* followed by a plain *Cort* well dug in.

"*My dearest,* and then *so anxious,*" said Clara, "and then the signature."

"He was at Fenbrook, she was in Europe with their boy. He probably wrote to her at odd moments every day," said Gamadge, "and often in pencil, as ideas occurred to him. His pencil was sharper at some times than it was at others, and he was quite unconscious of having left these facsimiles of his writing in this treasure of a book. Certainly he would never have laid his thin writing paper on a tissue guard again if he had seen what happened the first time he did so."

"And all we get," said Arline, "is that he was fond of his wife."

"We might have got more from the pages that were torn out. I think they were torn out the day they arrived at Number 24 from Fenbrook, or the next day; for on the next day, Friday the twenty-second, my client threw the first message to me out of the window. Four more messages were sent before I received the one Schenck brought me yesterday."

"Are you to find the picture?" asked Clara.

"My client doesn't want me to find it, but certain other people do, and one did; Mott Fenway."

"Did?"

"He doesn't want me to find it any more, because he died a few hours ago — just before I got to the house."

Clara and Arline gazed at him.

"He was killed, of course," said Gamadge, "so that he shouldn't set me to finding it."

"Henry —" Clara's eyes were fixed on him imploringly. "Don't go back to that house!"

"I shan't go back to find the picture."

"But if your client doesn't want it found, what does your client want you to do?" demanded Arline.

"I'm making a guess, and Harold, I think, has made the same one. I'm to get a young lady named Hilda Grove away from Fenbrook. She's a niece-by-marriage of Mrs. Fenway's companion and old school friend."

"Get her away! For how long?"

"I don't know; if I'm right at all about the case, an hour or so. But how does one persuade a young lady — an employee by the way — to leave a house without consulting her employers, without arousing comment on the part of two servants who are devoted to her, and without coercing or alarming her? Can you tell me?"

Arline said: "It doesn't seem such a hard kind of thing to do."

"Doesn't it? It's harder than you think. Harold is in the neighborhood, and he'll have to manage it tomorrow. He can't take her for a car ride, and have a breakdown, because there are no cars — pleasure driving is out. He can't lure her away on the pretext that somebody is hurt or ill, because she or the servants would communicate first with the Fenways. Harold and I met her this evening for the first time —"

"You've been up there?" exclaimed Clara.

"We have; and while she seemed to like us both very much she knows me at second hand and doesn't know anything about Harold at all, except that he's a Marine. He can't ask her to go for a walk in the snow; she wouldn't accept. If there were some outdoor sport to be used as an excuse, yes; a walk, no. Besides, a walk wouldn't last long enough. Nobody wants to walk in such weather. It's too cold."

They all sat in silence. Gamadge finished an apple, lighted a cigarette, and sank back against cushions, with his eyes shut. After an interval for thought Arline asked doubtfully: "Could I be a friend of an old school friend, and ask her to lunch somewhere?"

Gamadge replied gently, without opening his eyes: "No, Arline, you couldn't." He added: "Harold and I are the only new acquaintances she'll be able to assimilate for some time."

"Then what *am* I to do?"

"Er — liaison officer."

"Where?"

"The Oaktree Inn, half a mile this side of Fenbrook."

"When?"

"Tomorrow, if we ever succeed in getting Harold into that house up there."

Clara and Arline exchanged a blank look; but Gamadge suddenly rose to his feet, his

194

eyes gleaming and a smile on his lips. He said: "Let's all go down to the cellar."

They followed him nonplussed; into the hall, down by the elevator, to the kitchen precincts, and by an enclosed stairway to the furnace room. Gamadge turned on a light and paused to look with a jealous and appraising eye at his stock of coal; then he led them into a neat, dry, back cellar which was stacked with window screens and awnings, crates, and a collection of lumber. He opened a cupboard door.

"Things I am saving for my heirs," he said.

They saw skates, hockey sticks, a baseball bat, and a sled of the type known as a Flexible Flyer.

"Miss Grove has spent a considerable part of her youth in Switzerland," he continued. "There are snow-coved slopes in the vicinity of Fenbrook."

Clara was delighted. "Harold's to ask her to go coasting?"

"If he can tempt her."

"He could tempt *me!*"

"Operative Prady," said Gamadge, "will take this thing up to the Oaktree Inn tomorrow morning; not too irksome a task, I hope, and one which she will find easier if she tips liberally. She must spare no expense. She will deliver the flyer to Operative Bantz, who will take it to Fenbrook. She herself will register

195

at the Oaktree Inn, and remain there until further notice. She will treat herself to the best the house affords."

Arline received the Flyer from Gamadge, and lifted it. "It isn't heavy. Will they let me take it on the train?"

"Certainly they will. Don't go on to Rockliffe, you know; get out at the station below, and take a taxi to the Oaktree."

Clara spoke casually: "Arline, you'd better wear my thick tweed suit and topcoat. It may be awfully cold."

"I'll say I'll wear them."

"The sled is awfully dirty." Clara went off for dusters, and Gamadge took out his wallet. "Here's expense money now. I can't begin to say how grateful I am to you, Arline; the thing's in your hands now — yours and Harold's. Everything has to synchronize tomorrow, and I'll have to depend absolutely on you two. I'll call Harold up in the morning; let him know when I can leave my office for the Fenway house. Then he'll have to give me the all clear, and then I'll go up to Number 24 and try to give the all clear to my client."

"I'll do my part of it, anyway."

"Harold's job is going to be tough; I don't know how tough."

"Mr. Gamadge, excuse me for saying so, but you don't seem to know so very much about this case, do you?"

"The trouble is my client can't tell me much. Too dangerous."

Clara returned with cleaning rags, Gamadge found an oilcan, and they all dusted, polished and lubricated the Flyer until Gamadge pronounced it fit for service. He carried it up to the front hall, where Arline would find it in the morning. Arline then disappeared with Clara; when she came back she wore Clara's suit, topcoat and little tweed hat; Gamadge, closing the front door after her, remarked that she could now if necessary pass as the friend of a friend of Hilda Grove's.

"What's Hilda Grove like, Henry?"

"Inexpressibly lovely without and within."

"I don't see how she comes into this case at all." Gamadge, following her slowly up the stairs, said nothing, and she added, after a glance back at him, "I wish it was over."

"I think it will be over tomorrow."

13

CHILDISH

The manager of the Oaktree Inn was a little Austrian who had long considered himself immune to surprise; when, therefore, a taxi stopped under the porte-cochere on the morning of February 1st, and disgorged a young woman expensively dressed in English tweeds and hugging a large sled, he advanced to meet her with his accustomed mirthless smile. But another guest, who wore the uniform of a sergeant of Marines, reached the taxi first.

He greeted the wearer of the tweeds with moderate enthusiasm, and obtained permission from the manager to stow the Flexible Flyer in a lobby within a side door of the inn. Miss Prady meanwhile registered and was taken to her room.

The manager leaned on the desk to confide in the day clerk:

"I don't know anything about it any more. That hat and that ensemble came from a big house, but they were not made for her. And yet she is not a lady's maid. She and this Bantz are plain people, very plain people. Why does he bring her to this hotel? If he is spending his pay, why does he spend it here at this season, when the café is closed and there is no band?"

The clerk said sarcastically: "Local winter sports. Best they can do, with snow trains not running."

"Are they going to spend their time on a sled?"

But Harold and Arline spent their time until half past three o'clock with bourgeois propriety, eating a solid lunch and then sitting torpidly in front of the lounge fire. At half past three Harold was called to the telephone.

"I can start in half an hour," said Gamadge. "You'd better be on your way. Ring me up from there as soon as you find out whether she'll go. And keep her out for two hours; I want two hours. Be careful when you have the accident — pick a good soft drift. The Flyer's all right — I tested the ropes."

Harold had never done any coasting in his life; the sight of a sled reminded him of nothing more enjoyable than laborious efforts in his earliest youth to push himself over the black slush of mean streets. He felt that he was being asked to make a fool of himself now in a good cause, did not protest, and said merely that the Flyer looked O.K.

"I've changed my mind since I telephoned you this morning — about the isolating proposition. Where's that desk clerk, by the way?"

"Reading a funny paper."

"I said you'd better isolate as soon as you got there; the only trouble is that the people in the house may try to make a call and find out that something's wrong."

"No, they won't."

"Won't what? They might want to call the grocer."

"They can call anybody they like, but nobody will be able to get *them*. Didn't you know that if a telephone bell's out of order nobody knows it, not even the operator, till somebody gets mad at never getting an answer, and makes the company send up a repair man?"

"You don't say."

"They won't find out anything, or get a repair man, in two hours; more likely to be two weeks."

"Isolate as soon as you get there, then. I want to be able to tip the client off not only that H. G.'s off the place, but that the place is cut off."

"Half an hour, you'll hear from me."

Harold got the Flyer out of the inn and towed it up the driveway. The manager watched him go with a lacklustre eye.

"Doesn't even take her with him," he told

the desk clerk in colorless tones. "You might be wrong about them after all."

"I know nothing about such people; they don't belong in a starred hotel."

"We ain't in Baedeker now; we're in Rockliffe, N. Y." Harold towed the Flyer up the great waste of the Albany road; there was no traffic, and no contemptuous faces watched him from windows; the estates to right and left of the highway were placed well back among their own acres. Children of sledding age, he hoped, would not be at large so far from the village; but he did in fact acquire two passengers halfway to Fenbrook, and morosely dragged them and their sled uphill for a quarter of a mile.

A signpost, marked "Rockliffe Station," indicated the entrance to the narrow side road which had once been the Fenways' private lane. Harold followed the lane until a branch led him to the right; he went along a curving roadway walled in by evergreens, and presently found himself in front of the gray brick house.

Not a cheerful house; remote and cold even in the daylight, with patches of sun on its snowy yard. It was too tall and narrow, too long in the window, too shut away among its trees for cheerfulness. But Mrs. Dobson was certainly cheerful; she greeted him with a cry of welcome:

"If it ain't the sergeant, and a sled!"

"It was down at the inn; I thought Miss Grove might like to go coasting."

"She certainly will! Just the thing for her; she feels bad today. You didn't hear we had a bereavement?"

"You did? That's too bad."

"Mr. Blake called us this morning early; terrible accident. Mr. Mott fell out of his window in New York and was killed."

"That's a shame."

"Mr. Hendrix will be upset, won't he?"

"Oh — yes. I guess he will."

"Such a lovely gentleman. Miss Grove was so fond of him. They used to talk Swiss together. I'll go tell her you're here. Won't you come in?"

Harold left the Flyer on the drive, and waited alone in the cold hall. It was certainly not hard to get into Fenbrook, he told himself, and a minute later he found that it was not hard to get Miss Grove out of Fenbrook. She came running down the stairs in her green dress, flushed and eager.

"Sergeant Bantz, how perfectly wonderful of you! Where did you find that lovely sled?" She opened the front door to peep at it.

"It was at the inn."

"I'd love to go coasting! I'd adore to go! Only —" her face clouded. "Mrs. Dobson says she told you about Mr. Mott Fenway."

"Terrible."

"I wouldn't go coasting today, but he'd hate me to stay indoors. He'd think it was foolish, because I'm not a relation, and I really want to go."

"He had sense. You'd go for a walk, wouldn't you? I don't think," said Harold, smiling, "that this will be much different from a walk."

"If we go the way Bill Craddock took us once on a bobsled you'll think the walk back is rather strenuous," laughed Hilda. "That was something! There were four of us — Bill, and I, and Miss Fenway and a man friend of hers. We coasted straight from the top of that hill across the Albany Road, down the lane and right to the Rockliffe station! Around all the bends, and across the highways! And it was night. It won't be nearly so exciting today, I'm afraid, because it *isn't* night, and there's no traffic to be afraid of running into, and it's a small sled. Wait till I get my things on."

"May I telephone while you're doing it?"

"Of course."

Before he went into the telephone room Harold seized this opportunity to reconnoitre.

He opened the swing-door at the end of the hall, saw the rise of the back stairs, saw another swing-door on the right and heard Mr. Dobson's voice within. That seemed to be the kitchen. There was a laundry on the left, and cellar stairs beyond it were shut off by a door with a bolt on it. He saw that the bolt was shot back; he might need that cellar door later on; Gamadge's instructions had included orders to search the house. After the accident, of course; Harold's accident, which he must have while coasting. His lower lip protruded a little as he walked back to the telephone room. He did not much care to show himself up to Hilda Grove as a man who couldn't stick on a child's sled.

He called Gamadge at an unlisted address.

"O.K.," he said. "I'll have the subject out of this in ten minutes." He consulted his watch. "It's three after four."

"That's what I make it."

"Last call before I tackle the bell. Anything you want to add to the list?"

"Be sure you try to call me after you've made the search. Try Clara first; she'll relay to me at Number 24. Better for her to ring me there than for you to ring from where you are."

"You realize I may not be able to do a thing

until they're all tucked up for the night? That may mean breaking and entering. I can't stay myself; if I'm hurt as bad as that they'll send for a doctor."

"Do the best you can. You certainly ought to be able to make them let you shut yourself up in a bedroom and bath."

"How long do you think it takes to search a house?"

"Fifteen minutes ought to be enough, if there's anything seriously wrong there."

"It couldn't be anything but a —"

"No use guessing. I'm off. Good-bye."

Harold slowly replaced the receiver, and then got out a small tool kit. He extracted a screw driver from it and began to operate on the telephone box.

When he reappeared in the front hall Miss Grove was waiting for him in a skiing costume of unrelieved dark blue; color was provided by red mittens. They walked merrily off towing the Flyer, while Mrs. Dobson waved from the doorway.

They emerged from the lane, crossed the Albany Road, and climbed a long, low hill; it was cold, but there was no wind. At the top of the hill they looked beyond treetops to a yellowing sky.

Miss Grove knew how to stow herself economically on a sled; Harold had room to steer, and felt supported but not constricted by the firm grasp of her arms. They were off, and by the time they had shot across the highway and into the lane he had become aware of two things; their descent was going to be sensational, and it was lucky that Miss Grove was a veteran and knew how to use her feet. He wondered for a rushing moment whether the accident was going to be immediate and fatal, instead of later and a fake.

They rounded two turns without his quite knowing how, swept across the river road, and engaged the last slope without seeming to touch ground at all. He saw no reason to suppose that they would stop short of the Hudson — unless he was unable to steer clear of Rockliffe Station — and wondered if the ice would bear.

Hilda murmured in his ear: "Left."

He obeyed. They curved grandly to the left, ran along the road behind the station, slowed down and ceased to move.

"Wasn't it splendid?" asked Miss Grove.

Harold breathed deeply once or twice, and then looked over his shoulder; she was calm and smiling.

"Great," he said.

"You know, I think a Flyer is more sporting than a bob."

"I kind of think so myself."

"That run is worth the walk back, isn't it?"

"You bet."

On the walk back Harold tried to use his remaining faculties in picking out a place where he might have an accident and yet remain alive. He thought he remembered a high drift on the last turn before the lane entered the River Road; he did not think there was a stone wall under it. There had been no trees near it, either. Yes, there it was.

The second trip down was a nightmare in blue and white; but he made himself pull short on the last turn, and they entered the drift like bullets going into a bag of cotton waste. Hilda shot over his head; he sat shocked and immovable, his mouth full of snow.

When he backed out she was already on her feet and brushing herself off. He asked numbly: "Are you hurt?"

"Hurt? No! Of course not."

"Because I think I twisted my ankle."

Instantly she was all concern. "Oh, Harold, how ghastly. Is it bad?"

Harold staggered to his feet. He tested his left ankle, smiled courageously, and said he thought he could make it after he had rested a little; he sat down on the Flyer and got out his cigarettes.

"Oh *dear*," said Hilda; "you ought not to walk on it. Don't you think I'd better go somewhere and telephone for a car?"

"I bet I climb that hill easier than a car would."

"I'm not sure a car can climb it. It's all my fault; you weren't used to the run."

"Was Craddock used to the run?"

"He's done so much tobogganing."

"If I can't steer right I take the consequences. Have a cigarette. I'm glad I didn't bung you up, anyhow."

"I do hope it isn't a sprain."

Harold waggled his foot gently. "Don't think so. I'll strap it up when we get to the house." He added hastily: "If you have plaster. If not I can bandage it with a rag."

"We have lots of plaster."

"Then I'll be O.K."

"If I'd only had a chance to learn first aid!"

Harold said grimly: "I've learned it."

"On that island where the monkey was?"

"Nicest little feller you ever saw."

"Harold, when we do get back to the house you must let us send for the doctor. I won't risk having the rest of your leave spoiled."

"No doctor can fix me better than I can fix myself."

"Mrs. Dobson will be all upset. Anyway, you'll stay to supper?"

"Thanks. Oughtn't to impose on you."

Dusk fell, and stars were out in a cold sky,

before they reached the gray house. It was — Harold admired his own timing — five minutes past six. He managed an approach to Fenbrook from the rear, left the Flyer beside the kitchen porch, and clumsily trampled the snow in the yard. If he should be forced to come back and depart again late that night he would not leave a trail for Mr. Dobson to puzzle over.

Mrs. Dobson was at first full of reproaches; they had missed their tea, they would both have pneumonia, they had no sense. But when she noticed Harold's limp and heard the story of the accident, she was full of commiseration. She helped him off with his coat, Hilda meanwhile supporting him tenderly.

"What I say is," she declared, "if you go fast enough anything's dangerous, even a sled."

Harold gloomily agreed with her.

"I'll have supper ready for you both in no time. Are you sure you can fix that ankle so you can be comfortable on it, Sergeant?"

"Just give me the adhesive and a pair of scissors. It may take me some time."

"Dobson will help you."

"I'd rather do it myself."

Dobson was stoking the furnace, so Mrs. Dobson and Hilda helped the invalid upstairs and into a large front bedroom with an adjoining bath. Mrs. Dobson bustled about supplying him with a roll of plaster, a pair of shears, rubbing alcohol, surgical gauze and towels. They left him to himself.

He waited until Hilda had gone into her room to change; then, leaving the bedroom door closed behind him, dashed up the back stairs. He and Gamadge had agreed that the attic was the proper place to begin on, since Hilda had heard a squirrel there.

"Attic" was hardly the name for it; it was a ceiled, matchboarded northwest corner room, a neat repository for luggage and disused furniture. The trunks and boxes were not locked; was anything? Harold stood looking about him, his dark face lowering; he had the scientist's and technician's dislike of being hurried, and he had a bare quarter of an hour to search this attic.

Nothing to search except unlocked trunks and boxes, nothing but a corner cupboard which rose to the ceiling. He went over to it and turned the knob of its door; it was locked.

14

MEDIAEVAL

The late dusk of Eastern War Time still made it possible for Harold to do without his torch. It was a powerful one, and he did not care to light it until he could bury its gleam in the depths of a trunk or closet; Mr. Dobson might be out-of-doors on some errand to the garage, and might not only see a radiance behind the Holland shades, but notice that these were not pulled all the way down. Harold got out his tool kit again, and attacked the simple lock of the cupboard by twilight; the west window was only a few feet away.

The door swung open on loose hinges. What had Hilda Grove said last night? She had looked everywhere for the view of old Fenbrook except in one or two locked dress closets, locked since the family had moved to New York in the autumn. This must be one of them, but it was not full of summer clothing; it was empty, except for a square woolen knitting bag on one of its double row of hooks. The hooks were well above Harold's head, and the knitting bag — marked with enormous embroidered letters: *A.G.* — was hung where the two walls of the triangular cupboard met.

Mrs. Grove had not only left her bag behind her at Fenbrook, she had left work in it. Steel needles protruded from it, and it was bulging with a mass of yellow knitting and what looked like the contour of a ball of wool.

Harold wondered whether an illustration from a quarto might not be very well fit into Mrs. Grove's work-bag. He was about to satisfy himself on that point, but he was a slow thinker, trained to deliberation and accuracy. He always examined the outside of an object before he proceeded to its inner mysteries; but he never afterwards quite knew why he took his torch out of his pocket and turned it upon the interior of the closet before he stepped in. He turned the light of the torch upon ceiling, walls and floor — downwards, rather, because floor it had none.

He stood with one foot on the raised sill, gazing into a well of darkness; and his thoughts, when he began to have thoughts, proceeded in an orderly manner: Gamadge had argued that since the second arrow was not curved towards New York, Hilda Grove was not to be brought from Fenbrook to New York — she was simply to be removed from Fenbrook. Why, unless there were danger for her in Fenbrook? Harold was to look for the danger. He had found it, and Gamadge had been right.

Hilda Grove had told them — smiling — that one of the corner cupboards was not a china closet. Perhaps Gamadge would have been intelligent enough to realize that this corner cupboard was directly above one in the dining room; certainly he would now have agreed with Harold that a disused dumb-waiter might at one time have risen, in a house like Fenbrook, from the cellar to the top floor. When Fenbrook was built it had probably been heated by open fires only — hard coal, soft coal, wood for occasional fires on wet summer nights. A dumb-waiter would be almost a necessity for lifting hods and baskets of fuel to upper bedrooms.

But now there was a furnace, and the kitchen and laundry had been moved up from the basement to the first floor, and the dumb-waiter had been turned into cupboards by the simple process of fitting floors into it and supplying each section with hooks. From what Hilda Grove had said and intimated, the dining-room section had been left as it was.

Harold got down on his knees to examine the strong brackets that had been let into the brickwork of the wall. Triangular floorings had been made to fit, and apparently they

213

could be removed. He shifted to look behind him, and saw what he had seen before and passed over as unimportant — a triangle of wood that might have been a table top. It was behind a stack of awnings.

Above, in the ceiling of the cupboard, his torch showed him again the remains of lifting apparatus which no doubt had given him instinctive pause before he stepped into the void. To his death? He rather thought so; the drop to the floor of the cellar would be a long one. When he got up his knees were shaking — not from fear, but from a kind of horror. There was something so sly, so domestic about this trap, something so foreign to the place, the time, the sort of people who belonged in this house; yet one of them must have set it.

It had not been set for him, or for either of the Dobsons. It had been set for Hilda Grove; but if somebody telephoned or wrote her and asked her to get her aunt's knitting bag out of the attic cupboard and send it down to New York, she would need a key. She would be told where the key was. Certainly it would not be where Mrs. Dobson might find it by accident, but it would not be hidden far from the trap, or too deeply.

Harold found it in three minutes at the bottom of an old red scissors case, among oddments in the single drawer of a cherry-wood table; a table with a scarred top and a split leg. Not a table of distinction, not worth a cabinetmaker's bill for repairs.

Harold chose a mashie from a bag of old wooden golf clubs in a corner, and lifted the knitting bag off its hook. It contained nothing but a half-knitted sweater and a ball of wool. He stood holding it in his hand, unable to come to any decision as to his next step. He could replace the bag, lock the cupboard, and take away the key; that would leave the evidence intact, and no doubt make Hilda Grove quite safe; but he knew he could never leave Fenbrook while the trap remained as it was. He would have to consult Gamadge, and consult him directly.

He replaced the bag on its hook, replaced the golf club, and locked the cupboard door. He wanted violently to put the triangular flooring on its brackets, but restrained himself; at least he was in the house, and the telephone couldn't ring.

He went down the back stairs, listened, and then entered the bedroom below the attic. Here was a pseudo cupboard, locked. Harold unlocked it. Empty hooks here, no floor, brackets where the floor had been. He re-locked the door, and walked down the front stairs to the drawing room. Hilda was waiting for him in a rose-colored sweater and skirt; he apologized for his lateness — the bandage had been a little balky, but she could see that he wasn't limping.

"But you don't look a bit cheerful, Harold. Does it hurt you?"

"I'm O.K. I'll just stow the Flyer in your cellar till tomorrow."

"For goodness' sake let Mr. Dobson do it."

"Certainly I won't. You needn't come, I know where the steps are."

He pulled on his hat and coat and went out the back way. He carried the Flyer down the outside cellar stairs and through the first doorway to the left, into the original vast kitchen of Fenbrook. It had retained its old-fashioned range, but it was otherwise dismantled; all its windows were tightly locked and barred.

The dumb-waiter in the southwest corner was enclosed to a height of three feet, and above were double half-doors; when he opened them his torch shone on emptiness and a cement floor; the shaft rose unobstructed as far as his eye could reach.

He stepped back, closed the half-doors, and stood in the damp gloom feeling a sickness of the soul. Nobody who fell from the attic to that little shut-in space, and survived the fall, would be heard — or found — for a long time.

Why must this girl die? And how, he asked himself, could the accident be explained later? Unless Mrs. Grove or her accomplice intended to remove the body, replace the floorings above, and contrive some other explanation for Hilda's death. "Niece-by-marriage," growled Harold, and muttered some epithets uncomplimentary to Mrs. Grove. If he did not call her an unnatur'd hag it was because he was not familiar with *King Lear*. But it was the thought of Craddock that staggered him, the possibility — probability, he told himself — that Craddock was Mrs. Grove's agent. Such people didn't exist now; they had lived once, if he could believe history; they and this oubliette belonged together, might have existed in the middle ages, perhaps even as late as the eighteenth century. There was cruelty now, deception now, murder for a price; but what price could repay Craddock for a deed like this?

He knew very well that such crimes *were* possible today; no use fooling himself.

When he reached the back hall again by way of the inner stairs Mrs. Dobson popped her head out of the kitchen to tell him that supper was ready.

"I just have to put in a call."

He went into the telephone room and called the Gamadge house. Clara answered: "He must be at Number 24, Harold. He hasn't come home. Shall I try to get him there, and give him a message?"

"Think I'll try myself."

He rang the Fenway house, and the voice that answered caused him to mumble his next question: "Mr. Blenker in?"

"You got the wrong number," said the voice of an unmistakable policeman. "Some people just can't learn to dial."

Harold, standing fixed in front of the telephone, thought that nobody down there would bother with this call, trace it or even report it. After a moment he called the Oaktree Inn; if he must go to New York, Arline would have to be insinuated somehow into Fenbrook. But the clerk informed him to his rage that Miss Prady was not on the premises.

"Certainly she's there," he insisted. "Page her."

"She went out a little while ago."

Harold slammed the receiver down, picked it up, and ordered a taxi for the next down train. "I'll have to chance it," he said to himself. "Liaison's busted, and something's evidently breaking down there; but I'll have to chance somebody coming up here in the next couple of hours or sending a telegram."

He went into the dining room, but the sight of food did not allure him; he would have liked a drink, and was sorry to infer that Hilda did not think it proper to supply her own private guests with Fenway whiskey. He longed to blow the thing to her, but he could not; somehow, he furiously hoped, she might be spared the knowledge of that trap in the attic. He hoped she might never know about it at all.

The doorbell rang, and Harold leapt from his chair. He was in the hall before Mrs. Dobson had come out of the kitchen, and flung the door open; he was quite ready to receive Mr. Craddock, but it was not Craddock who stood in the dark of the porch.

15

THE ALL CLEAR

At approximately four minutes past four o'clock that afternoon Gamadge turned from the telephone to address a small man in dark spectacles. The office was a cubbyhole, part of a series on the twentieth floor of a building that overlooked Bowling Green.

"Well," he said, "that's settled then. You people won't send any more letters to our friend, or any letters through that route at all."

The small man looked anxious. "I hope he is in no serious trouble."

"He may have been transferred before they decoded us."

The small man shook his head.

"Anyhow," and Gamadge handed a folder across his desk, "you can tell them definitely in Room 7 that Doumets didn't write this. There's no tremor, they couldn't reproduce that even if they knew it was there."

"They might have known it would be there!"

"They couldn't reproduce it; otherwise the forgery's almost perfect. You were very clever to suspect it."

"There was something in the tone of it."

"They couldn't reproduce that, either — the incalculable factor. I've put the enlarged photographs in the folder too. Room 7 will take charge. I'm awfully sorry, Georges."

The small man rose. "What your office has saved in lives! But not this one, I am afraid, Mr. Gamadge; not this one."

"I don't feel very effective, sometimes, in an office."

"No; but all of us cannot act. We must do what we can."

They shook hands, and Gamadge conducted him to the door. Then he put on his hat and coat, took the real right *Elsie Venner* and the book of views under his arm, and went into action himself.

The subway took him to within a few blocks of the Fenway house. He arrived there on foot, went up the front steps, and rang. No outmoded wreath or crape was on the door, none was needed; everybody knew by this time what had happened here last night.

Phillips, very mournful, said that Miss Fenway expected Mr. Gamadge, and was allowed to take *Elsie Venner* from him for careful disposition in the library; Gamadge retained the other book, and waited for Caroline in the drawing room.

He stood in front of the high mantel, looking up at a full-length portrait of some lady, probably Blake Fenway's mother. Her exquisite face looked down at him with the suggestion of a smile, but it was only a polite smile. Her elbows were close to her sides in what was certainly a characteristic pose; her hands held a tiny fan. She rose from the waist out of a billowing surge of stiff pearl-colored satin, her neck rose from a standing ruche like frozen foam. Her head was drawn back a little; reserved she was, not timid: he did not think she had liked sitting for her portrait.

Caroline said behind him from the doorway: "How do you like Grandmamma Fenway, Mr. Gamadge?"

He turned. "Better than she would have liked me."

"I believe that she was rather difficult to live up to. I gather that she was formidable, but what a beauty! You ought to see the picture of the girl she is said to have wanted for Uncle Cort."

"Not the kind of girl he chose for himself?"

"Oh, never anything but white-muslin party dresses until she came out, and black shoes. *She* had no matchmaking mamma, so she withered on the parent stem. What's that you have? The book of views?"

"Yes. It's most interesting, even in its present faulty condition. Shall we look at it?"

They went into the back drawing room, and Caroline bent over the marked pages. "What on earth, Mr. Gamadge?"

"Indecipherable, almost, without a reading glass, but I think you will be able to make out your Uncle Cort's signature."

"Yes, here it is, quite plain. How extraordinary. He wrote a letter and it came through."

"Valid, I should think, in a court of law, but I should like counsel's opinion. It's a nice point, isn't it?"

"It's very like him to have marked up a book in this way through pure absent-mindedness. So kind and considerate, you know, but very casual and easy-going. I remember him so well. He'd never knowingly deface a book, of course. He'd . . ." she looked up, suddenly startled. "Good gracious."

"What is it?" Gamadge smiled at her.

"*I've* thought of a nice point! Suppose that he wrote a letter which for some reason he afterwards decided not to send after all; something he couldn't send, and tore up; and then suppose he found marks on the book, and knew they wouldn't rub out!"

"Quite a dilemma for him."

"He must have been frightfully tempted to tear the page out, but I can't imagine him doing it without telling Father. And Uncle Cort wouldn't have torn out the picture and then preserved it."

"But if it is in existence, who doesn't want me to find it?"

She stood perplexed and rather frightened. "Aunt Belle certainly isn't hunting for it; she can't get about except in that wheel chair. And she couldn't make Alden understand how to look for it and what to look for. Mr. Gamadge — these marks put a different complexion on the whole thing. Have I been wrong about Alden?"

"I never thought that Alden Fenway tore out the picture; I never thought it the act of a mental deficient."

"He wouldn't have understood these marks."

"No."

"But if I've been wrong about Alden, I may have been wrong about Cousin Mott's death too. Could it have been an accident after all?"

Gamadge said nothing.

"Uncle Mott and I were so frightfully prejudiced. I should hate to think that we . . . Mr. Gamadge!"

"Yes?" Gamadge smiled at her.

"Perhaps we'd better drop the whole thing."

"People are always doing this to me, Miss Fenway."

"Doing what?"

"Asking me to find something out for them, and then regretting the impulse."

"It's only that these marks make it all look so different."

"Your father wouldn't have called my attention to the missing picture if he'd torn it out himself, you know."

"Torn it out himself? Ridiculous!" Caroline's dark eyes tried to meet his squarely.

"I thought you might be wondering how far he'd go to preserve his brother's posthumous reputation."

For the first time he could see a resemblance in her to her grandmother Fenway; the withdrawn look, the poise of the head as she drew in her chin to glance upwards at him. "He'd do nothing wrong for any reason. I thought you might have some wild idea —"

"I never have them; it's you who had the wild idea, and you must abandon it."

"I never had it. *Fenways* aren't capable of lying and cheating to preserve the family reputation!"

Gamadge privately thought that Grandmother Fenway had probably been capable of almost anything; he had a shocking mental picture of that lady taking a slim hand from her fan to push a troublesome relative-by-marriage out of a window. But she of course was not by blood a Fenway. He said: "Let me assure you that I have no dark suspicions of your father. When he and I discussed the lost picture he did so without knowing that there was a present mystery connected with it. He certainly didn't know that Mr. Mott Fenway was going to consult me about it later, or that you were going to do so."

She stood with her eyes on the mansion of J. Delabar King. "It will upset him, all this about Uncle Cort writing these letters and leaving these marks. I wish he needn't know."

"Don't you shelter him too much?"

"You needn't laugh at me."

"I'm not laughing."

"It's his own fault if I do, poor darling, he's so sensitive. Mr. Gamadge, I've had another thought."

"A pleasant one?"

"A perfectly horrible one, but at least it doesn't involve *us*. I mean it's nothing Father would *die* of. Suppose Mrs. Grove found the marks, and read them, and tore the picture and the tissue out? And is blackmailing Aunt Belle?"

"What could Mr. Cort Fenway have written

that his widow can be blackmailed about?"

"Something he discovered, something she'd done. But then he couldn't bear to send the letter, he decided to wait until he saw her again. But he never did see her again — he died."

"I thought they were devoted."

"It must have been something she did before they were married."

"No chance afterwards?"

"Oh, no; they were inseparable until he had to leave her with Alden and come to America on business. Even I admit that she loved him."

"Mrs. Grove isn't blackmailing her about Alden, then, but about her own past? Mrs. Fenway's past?"

"It's all I can think of, if you're right about a letter of Uncle Cort's having been on the picture."

"You think that rather than have her blackmailing game spoiled, rather than have the picture found, Mrs. Grove pushed your cousin Mott Fenway out of the window?"

Caroline was again shocked and startled. "Deliberate murder? I never thought it was that!"

"Your father wouldn't like it to come out, would he?" Gamadge looked at her with enquiry in his eye.

"If it was deliberate murder of course it

must come out!"

Was there so much of Grandmother Fenway in Caroline, after all? Grandmother Fenway would certainly have hushed up a family murder. Blake Fenway, Gamadge thought, would be strongly tempted to hush one up. Was Caroline not even tempted? The old tradition seemed to be waning.

He picked up the book of views. "I'll just put this back in the coffer," he said, "and then we can go upstairs and proceed with our investigation."

"You'll find out nothing from Aunt Belle or Mrs. Grove; they're quite themselves again."

"I shall be interested in seeing them, though."

They crossed to the library, and Gamadge replaced the book of views in the inlaid casket. Caroline glanced about her. She asked: "Are you going to try to find the picture?"

"I must admit that I'm getting a better notion of where to look for it."

"It will be easier to find if Alden didn't hide it; a child's mind works so illogically. Mr. Gamadge — are you going to look here? An endless job, I should think, with all these books!"

"To tell you the truth, I'd much rather your father found it for himself."

She said quietly: "That's nice of you. But you'll tell him where to look?"

"Perhaps it won't be necessary for me even to do that. I wonder if you would try to give me the run of the house after we leave the sitting room? Would it seem too strange to Phillips or another servant if I were discovered mooning about on the stairs?"

"I'm not to be with you?"

"Well, no; I shan't involve you in my activities, Miss Fenway. Wash your hands of me. Play the piano."

"Play the piano? You mean it?"

"I'll listen for the notes of that Bach fugue I saw on the rack last night."

Caroline looked at him wonderingly. "I feel rather as I did at the childrens' party when the conjuror told me to look at the card in his hand, and then took it out of my pocket."

"My sleeves are rolled up too, I assure you."

"There is something a little tense about you."

"Is there? I'm sorry I show it."

They came out of the library, went along the hall, and mounted the stairs. Gamadge said: "It's a quiet house. Absorbs sound."

"I've begun to hate it. I should look forward to getting out of it, except that when I do my father will be dead."

They reached the square landing over which

229

Psyche presided in her niche, and stepped from it to the wide upper hall. The house did absorb sound; hardly a murmur of voices came from the open doorway of the sitting room, although when they entered they found five people there. A tea table was set out at the far end of the hearth, and Phillips in Caroline's absence was dispensing tea and cakes. Mrs. Grove sat beside the tray, Alden next her behind the round worktable, and Mrs. Fenway in her wheel chair just within the doorway. The extension of the chair had been folded in, and the end of it formed a step for her feet. The silk robe lay across her knees.

Alden was working at a cardboard puzzle, and did not look up from it; Craddock, in the bay window, returned Gamadge's nod and then looked out into the street again.

Caroline said: "Here's Mr. Gamadge, come to bring Father his books. I persuaded him to come up and have tea."

Mrs. Fenway turned her head to smile at him, and put her hand up to the level of her shoulder. "I'm so glad," she said.

Gamadge took the hand, released it — it was feverishly hot — and bowed to Mrs. Grove, who had glanced up as he came in. She bowed in return, and lowered her eyes again to her needlework.

Mrs. Fenway said: "You're just in time,

Phillips was going to clear away," and patted the back of the chair between her and the hearth. Caroline had already established herself in the one she had occupied the day before, and was pouring tea for herself and the guest. Phillips brought Gamadge his cup and plate.

Gamadge drank, his eyes on the small creature opposite him who worked so busily; why did Caroline, he wondered, think that *she* was "quite herself again?" She was like a listening small animal of the woods. He noted the rounded forehead of obstinacy, the set lips. Her well-shaped head under its plain bands of iron-gray hair showed intellect. Neutral in her gray dress she sat effaced, but Gamadge thought that Mrs. Grove dominated the scene as a rock dominates a bright landscape.

Craddock had at last decided to join the group. He came up behind Alden, touched his shoulder, and said: "Here's a visitor, old man."

Alden looked up with his amiable, vacant smile. He said: "You did come back."

"But not for long. I must swallow my tea and go. I'm on the wing."

"I'm running out myself to get stamps. I hope you'll be here when I come back?" Craddock met Gamadge's eyes.

"Afraid not. Some other time, I hope?"

231

Craddock nodded and went off. Caroline said: "We came up to see you last night, Aunt Belle, but you had gone to bed."

"The doctor told us this morning. I was so sorry. They've told me, Mr. Gamadge, how kind you were last night. Our first tea without dear Mott, I'm glad you're with us to fill his place. We miss him so."

"I miss him," said Gamadge, "after only one meeting."

A gasping note had come into her voice. "Who wouldn't? I remember him so well as a young man, but of course he was much older than the rest of us. We all looked up to him as a wonderful, learned person, but he was such a beautiful dancer too, and loved parties. I remember him so well at parties. He used to dance with me, and I was so flattered — a Harvard graduate, so old! He used to hold my hand up straight with my fan in it, while I clutched my dress up with the other hand, you know; he held my fan up and pointed at people with it when he said funny things about them. So silly, but we laughed. He was part of our lives, it's a chapter closed, he's been spared all sorts of awful things. Old age, illness, all the misery."

Alden looked up at her, a slight frown on his smooth forehead and an enquiring expression in his eyes.

"It's all right, darling." She smiled at him, and then went on in the gasping voice that had disturbed him: "I'm just a little nervous. It's all right. He knows when I'm nervous, Mr. Gamadge, and it upsets him so; I must control myself better. But I keep thinking of last night. Here we sat, just where we are now, the three of us, after Bill went out of the room. We were going to play bridge, Blake said he'd play. Just tiny stakes you know, to make it more fun. One *can't* go through all the work and suspense, can one, and then not even bother to add the scores up? And Bill Craddock would gamble with his last penny, and Mrs. Grove likes a gamble too; don't you, Alice?"

The question was put a trifle diffidently. Mrs. Grove said without raising her eyes that she had had English parents, who put something on a game as a matter of course.

"Such sports, aren't they, and the racing too." Her breathless voice went on: "We do seem provincial compared with them in so many ways. But kind, I think we're kind. Well, here we sat, and the next thing we knew was when Phillips came and knocked at Caroline's door. He was terribly shaken, but Phillips is considerate and careful; he told me privately — that Cousin Mott had gone away, Alden. You remember? I told you all about it afterwards."

"But he didn't take his coat and hat." Alden looked mildly puzzled. "I saw them in the closet downstairs this morning."

Mrs. Fenway laughed and patted his hand. "*You* have two coats and two hats, you silly boy; why shouldn't he?"

Caroline said: "Have you really finished your tea, Mr. Gamadge? Then we all have, Phillips, and you may clear away."

Phillips gathered cups and plates. A calm domestic scene, which Caroline kept on the same level with her next question: "Have you had an interesting day? But all your days must be interesting, of course."

Gamadge accepted a cigarette from Mrs. Fenway's box, lighted it at the silver lamp Phillips presented to him, and answered: "Unusually interesting. Exciting. I suppose I may tell you that I see a good many people in the course of my day's work who are in touch with friends in prison camps abroad."

"Oh, do you?"

"Yes, and sometimes my office gets indirectly into touch with them, though I don't always even know who they are. One of my clients, for instance, has a friend who was interned a little distance away from a large city; this afternoon I found, after having sent and received a number of code messages, that we had been able to get my client's friend out."

Phillips had gone, and except for the small click and rattle of the colored marbles in Alden Fenway's game, the room was quiet.

"Actually out of the prison camp?" asked Caroline.

"Yes, and more than that; we had arranged to cut communications. The telephone was put out of commission for at least an hour and a half. And how do you think we arranged to get the party away from the place?"

"How?" Mrs. Fenway gazed at him.

"On a sled. We had a cable; and at this moment my client can be sure that the party is coasting down a hill on a sled. Not an unusual diversion, you know, even for grown people."

"But when will you know the final result?" Caroline was interested.

"Oh — never, perhaps. That's my client's business now; my part of the job is over. But if my client should need my further services, I can easily be got into touch with again."

"What wonderful things you do."

Gamadge thought: She won't speak while I'm here. She's waiting for Fenway. I'd better go. He rose, and said: "You'll all forgive me, I hope; I must fly."

Caroline rose too. "You won't wait for Father? He ought to be here any moment now."

"I really can't. Don't ring, I can let myself out."

Mrs. Fenway extended her hot hand, she gave him a last quivering smile; Mrs. Grove lifted her inscrutable face, and the pinched mouth curved upwards. Alden Fenway, engrossed with the colored balls and the cardboard box, did not raise his head.

As Gamadge left the room he told himself that it was magnificent and terrifying. "There she sits, and the other woman's oblivious; doesn't know the game is up. I mustn't be too far away."

But first he went downstairs, waited a minute, and then opened and closed the front door. He retreated to the passage that concealed the back stairs; Phillips could be heard clinking china in the pantry, the coast was clear. He lingered until the rippling notes of the Bach fugue reached him; Caroline was playing away as though her life depended on it. Thankful that she was well away from the storm centre, he ran up to the second floor.

16

BLOODSHED

Gamadge went through into the main hall, and keeping well to the left edged his way as far as Caroline's bedroom. He backed in, and drew the door to a crack; he could see nothing of the group in front of the fire, but he could hear what they said. Mrs. Fenway was speaking: "... warn you for the last time that we've come to the end of this."

Mrs. Grove replied harshly: "You've said that before."

"But this time I mean it. You made a great mistake when you thought that you could keep me in this state of torture forever."

"It was for you to end it."

"You inhuman creature, do you think nobody has any brains but yourself? I have no pity for you, you have no heart. You don't know what it is to have a child. But it's all over."

Gamadge heard the front door slam. He thought: Somebody came in with a key, that must be Fenway.

Mrs. Grove said: "You can't frighten me with these threats, Belle."

Mrs. Fenway's voice rose: "That was Blake. Alice — one more chance — only one! Why must you think of the money? So stupid, so cruel!" Her voice changed. "What are you looking at me like that for? What are you going to do?"

"End it." Mrs. Grove sounded nearer, as if she had risen from her chair and stepped forward. "End it now."

The sitting-room door moved, and then slammed as Gamadge dashed from Caroline's room to hurl himself against it; he heard the lock turn. There was a shot, a scream, another shot, and silence. Gamadge whirled to see Blake Fenway standing transfixed at the head of the stairs.

"Through Alden's room," shouted Gamadge, as he ran past Fenway and swung to the left. "This way."

Fenway was at his heels as he raced through Alden's bedroom, Mrs. Grove's room and the bath, and then across Mrs. Grove's room to the other doorway. There they both stopped.

Mrs. Fenway lay back against the cushions of her chair, mouth open and eyes closed. Blood streamed through the fingers of her right hand, which clasped her wounded left wrist. Alden Fenway stood leaning across the round table, looking down at something on the floor; there was a stupid, frightened, guilty look on his face. He held a little automatic pistol loosely in his right hand, as if he did not know that he was holding it at all. Mrs. Grove lay face downwards in front of the fireplace, blood spreading fanwise from her head and soaking into the hearthrug.

Blake Fenway spoke hoarsely over Gamadge's shoulder: "Great God, what's happened?"

Alden stammered: "She hurt Mother. She — she hurt Mother."

Gamadge went over to the dead woman, knelt, and turned her on her back. She had been shot full in the forehead. Her glazing eyes stared beyond him as though even in death she avoided his own. Her small face looked pinched and severe.

He got up, lifted the silk robe from Mrs. Fenway's knees, and covered the body. Then he went around the table and took the little automatic from Alden's fingers; he slipped the safety catch and handed the gun to Fenway. Fenway had come up to take his nephew by the arm.

"My boy," he asked in a broken voice, "why did you do this?"

"I didn't mean to. She hurt Mother."

Gamadge asked: "Got a clean handkerchief, sir?"

Fenway, still keeping his nervous hold on Alden's arm, fumbled in a pocket with his other hand and produced a white square. Gamadge took out his own handkerchief and went over to Mrs. Fenway. He gently drew her fingers from her hurt wrist, examined the flesh wound, and began to construct a tourniquet with the help of his own fountain pen.

Fenway said: "She ought to — we must get a doctor."

"If you'll find some water in that bathroom, sir?"

Mrs. Fenway opened her eyes. She looked at the bandage on her arm, at Gamadge, at her brother-in-law. "Blake!"

"For God's sake, Belle, what happened?"

"She shot me, she would have killed me, but Alden was on her like lightning. I never knew what she was going to do until she had shut and locked the door and got that pistol out of her bag. Alden snatched the pistol away from her and put it up to her forehead. Did he — is she dead?"

"I'm afraid so."

"Will they put him in prison for saving my life?"

"Prison? No!"

There was a loud knocking at the door.

Gamadge said: "I'll attend to it, Mr. Fenway, if you'll get that water. And you'd better lock the door from the bathroom."

Fenway turned blindly away. Gamadge opened the door and confronted Caroline; she was very white. Old Phillips and a woman servant stood behind her. She asked loudly: "Where's Father? I saw him go up. What's the matter?"

"Mrs. Grove has been killed."

"Mrs. Grove?"

"And your aunt has been shot in the arm. We're calling the police, of course. Your father won't want you in this room, Miss Fenway; will you round the servants up downstairs?"

Still staring, she backed dumbly away. Gamadge closed the door and locked it; he turned to find Blake Fenway approaching his sister-in-law's chair, a tumbler of water in his hand. Gamadge took it from him and held it to Mrs. Fenway's lips. When she had swallowed some of it, he put the glass down and looked at her.

"If you can stand this for a few minutes," he said, "I think you'd better try. It will be much easier for the police and for all of us if the room is as it was when the death occurred."

"I can stand anything. I want to tell the police what happened."

241

Alden was looking from one to another of them, his eyes returning again and again to the stained fingers of his mother's right hand. Fenway clasped him around the upper arm once more. "Come over to the window, my boy. Come and look out of the window."

"They don't let me!"

"You can do it today."

"But it's getting dark."

Fenway, distractedly looking about him, asked: "Where's Craddock? Why doesn't Craddock come?"

"He went to the post office, Blake," said Mrs. Fenway. "Alden, you know you like to see the lights." Her voice broke, and then she was crying spasmodically.

Alden walked slowly to the bay, and turned a chair to face the east window. He sat down with his back to the room, pulled aside a white glass-curtain, and peered out towards the avenue.

Fenway leaned over his sister-in-law. "You must tell us, Belle, before we send for people. What in God's name did she shoot you for?"

"I think she's been going mad, Blake." Mrs. Fenway was controlling her sobs. "I think losing her house and her money, all she had, and the terrible anxiety, and the journey — it's all driven her mad by degrees. She often said that life wasn't worth living to her if she had to be dependent in her old age, and that she couldn't face it. I told her we'd take care of her — Alden and I, you know; I thought Alden's estate might be willing to pension her if she acted as our housekeeper when we *had* a house. She knew how little money *I* had. Lately, about a week and a half ago, she began to demand money from me. A hundred thousand dollars. She said I must raise it in cash, and take it and go away."

"A hundred thousand dollars?"

"I was to make up some story to get it from you, or sell everything I had of my own. She said that if I breathed a word to you or to anyone Hilda would be killed."

"*Hilda?*"

"She said there was some kind of trap at Fenbrook, and that if she telephoned, Hilda would set it off or walk into it or something and be killed. She said that she could get to a telephone because she had a pistol; that if I told she would have nothing to lose, and that she'd kill me and then herself. I thought she was mad, but how could I risk the danger to Hilda?"

"You must have realized that she was raving! You should have managed to tell us somehow."

"It wasn't easy; she was always there. How could I risk it? I've dreamed of that telephone.

I could hear it ringing at Fenbrook, and then I could see Hilda answering it."

"It was only a threat, Belle. How long has this been going on, did you say?"

"For more than a week. I thought Alice was getting very strange and silent, and then suddenly one day she burst out with it. She knows how fond of Hilda I am."

"This is horrible. When could she have set a trap at Fenbrook?"

"I don't think she can have gone up there secretly at night, but I don't know. Perhaps she did it — if there is a trap — before we came down last summer."

Fenway cast a shrinking and incredulous look at the figure outlined by the silk robe. He said: "Horrible. Were we to find this trap after she went away?"

"She was going to leave it until she did get safely off; she said she knew where to go. And then she was going to write me what it was and how to find it."

"I don't for one moment believe that there's anything wrong at Fenbrook. What made her turn on you today?"

Tears began to roll again down Mrs. Fenway's ashen face. "Oh, Blake, I was afraid she'd killed Mott, and I couldn't stand it any longer."

Fenway staggered back a step or two, and

caught hold of the edge of the table. "Killed — Mott!"

"I was afraid he'd somehow found out what she was doing to me, and that she killed him last night to prevent his telling you."

"But my God, Belle, you said she was with you here last night!"

"She made me; I've been such a coward! But it couldn't go on, she was too dangerous; she might have murdered you or Caroline. I was going to call to you when you came upstairs and ask for help. I hoped she'd give way when it came to the point, and that perhaps she had no pistol after all. But she got up and said very well, she'd end it herself, and took the pistol out of her bag and shut and locked the door. If I'd only known Mr. Gamadge was there! I could have screamed for *him*. I didn't know my poor boy would be the one to save me! Blake, he was so frightened when he'd fired at her; he went around the table and stood staring at her; he didn't even know what he'd done. Blake, they oughtn't to touch him for this!"

"Belle, my poor Belle, do you think I'd let anyone maltreat him?"

Gamadge said: "We must telephone now. Shall I do it, sir? The doctor first for Mrs. Fenway. What's his number?"

Fenway supplied the number, and Gamadge

called Thurley's office. His secretary said that the doctor had gone home, and that she would relay the call and send him immediately to Number 24. Then Gamadge called the precinct.

"Get Nordhall," begged Fenway. "He's a decent, intelligent fellow. Get Nordhall."

Gamadge succeeded after some difficulty in getting Nordhall, and heard his name repeated inquiringly by that calm official voice.

"You saw me at the Fenways' last night," said Gamadge.

"Oh yes. Friend of the family."

"There's some more trouble at the Fenways'; I'm calling from there."

"Kind of trouble?"

"Mrs. Grove has been shot and killed."

The calm voice roughened. "Mrs. Grove? Mrs. Fenway's companion? You said killed?"

"By Alden Fenway."

"What?"

"And Mrs. Fenway's wounded in the arm. Explain when you get here."

"Where's young Fenway now? What's he doing?"

"Looking out of the window."

"Be with you. Don't move anything."

"The whole party is in the room where the shooting occurred, and Mr. Fenway and I are here too — we got here a half minute afterwards — and both doors are locked."

"Hold it that way."

When Gamadge looked up from the telephone, Blake Fenway stood at his elbow. "Mr. Gamadge," he said, and all the kindness of his nature expressed itself in the words, "that child up at Fenbrook; I must let her know."

Gamadge rose. "You'll want to speak to her yourself, sir."

"I don't know how to tell her; what to say."

Mrs. Fenway's eyes were again closed. She said faintly: "Don't tell her everything; just say — just say it was an accident."

Fenway asked for the Fenbrook number, waited for some time, and then looked up at Gamadge in surprise. "They say the house doesn't answer."

Gamadge, leaning against the edge of the table, looked sympathy.

"I don't understand it; the Dobsons never leave the place completely empty, never. Something must be wrong with the wires — all this bad weather. It's unfortunate; they telephone telegrams, and I dare say a messenger wouldn't be available for hours, if at all. It's a long way from the village, the roads must be deep in snow. I shall have to telephone the station to send a taxi up with a note. I suppose he can leave it in the door; Hilda — it's really too bad."

"You might send somebody up from here."

Fenway glanced at his sister-in-law's face, and back at Gamadge. He lowered his voice. "Might the police object? I know how strict they are, even when it's a plain case of — of mental incompetence. Gamadge, it's the end of him." He nodded towards the hunched figure in the window. "They'll put him away for life."

"I think they will." Gamadge also spoke below his breath.

"Tragedy. But this poor child at Fenbrook — after what Belle told us, that incredible story about a trap in the house up there, I won't have Hilda Grove spend another night in the place until it's been searched. A trap? What kind of trap? Gamadge, the thing's a nightmare."

"I happen to know a young woman who's spending the night at the Oaktree Inn. Isn't that near Fenbrook?"

"Only a bare half mile; but it's — I really couldn't ask —" Fenway's eyes lightened.

"She'll be glad to walk up, and if necessary she'll bring Miss Grove to New York herself."

"I cannot tell you how it would relieve my mind. The Dobsons, good people, are quite unequipped to deal with such a difficult situation. Hilda will be distracted; a loyal, affectionate child. She seemed really to love this

248

— this —" he shook his head. "But the woman was out of her mind."

Gamadge called the Oaktree Inn, and got Miss Prady on the wire. He said: "Arline? I have a great favor to ask of you . . . Thanks, I know you will if you can. There's a Miss Grove staying at a place called Fenbrook, half a mile up the road —"

"Tell her there's a sign at the lane," said Fenway, "but she must have a taxi and charge it to me."

"You're to take a taxi, and charge it to Fenway. Get that? Fenway. Er — Mr. Fenway is here beside me now. There seems to be something the matter with the Fenbrook telephone, he can't get the house. There's been a fatality here, Miss Grove's aunt has been killed. Can you break it to her, say it was an accident, and get her down to New York by the first possible train? I know it's a lot to ask, but . . . Thank you, Arline, I knew you would."

He laid the receiver down; if he could have been amused at anything just then he would have been amused at Arline's superhuman behavior; after his warning she had braced herself to receive the staggering news with the polite sympathy that Fenway would expect from a total stranger; Gamadge really did not know how she had managed it.

The front doorbell rang twice. Fenway turned to his sister-in-law. "Belle, my poor Belle, here they are. A few minutes more and you'll be under Thurley's care, and in bed. You ought to have been there long ago. You're magnificent."

She opened her eyes. "Nothing could make me leave Alden until I know what they mean to do."

"Don't be afraid. I shall be here and Thurley will be here; and Gamadge will help us make them understand."

"I'm glad he stayed." She said faintly: "I know they'll take Alden to a hospital; I'm prepared for that."

"Then you have nothing at all to worry about."

Alden turned to look at them. He said: "I like the hospital."

Gamadge went and unlocked the door. As he opened it Nordhall, followed by uniformed men, advanced along the hall, and the expression on his face was indescribable.

17

WHY NOT BE FRANK?

Lieutenant Nordhall's eyes were of the shade once fashionable as Iceberg Blue, and held no warmth; but from the moment — shortly after six o'clock — when he arrived in the Fenway sitting room he behaved with consideration, even with sympathy. He listened to Mrs. Fenway's tragic story, and heard Gamadge's and Fenway's description of the scene that had met their eyes when they halted in the bedroom doorway. He complimented her on her courage in waiting where she was to see him, assured her that her son would be treated not as a criminal but as an invalid, and allowed Thurley — who stood fuming beside her — to have a nurse put her to bed. The nurse had arrived as soon as Thurley's own car could bring her from his pet hospital; but neither she nor Thurley could force Mrs. Fenway to take a sedative until Alden's fate should have been settled and reported to her.

Alden, rather bewildered-looking but docile, had been taken to his own room under the surveillance of a plain-clothes policeman; Craddock, who came back to the house and learned the news at half past six, immediately went up and battered at the door. He insisted violently on being with his patient, and was allowed to see him. Satisfied when he found no handcuffs on Alden's wrists, and no signs of police coercion other than the plain-clothes man's attempt to teach Alden beggar-my-neighbor, Craddock at last consented to be questioned mildly himself.

Mrs. Grove's body was taken away. Pale and trembling servants rolled up the rug from in front of the fireplace, removed the cushions from Mrs. Fenway's chair and the silk coverlet that Gamadge had used as a pall, and wrapped them for the cleaners. Craddock, aided by police, dealt as best he could with the press. A crowd — this time a really considerable crowd — gathered in front of the house. The commissioner of police and an assistant district attorney called, saw Blake Fenway, conversed with Nordhall, and went away again. By half past seven the house was quiet, and Nordhall, stimulated by a cup of coffee, had time to hold a parting conference with four persons in the back drawing room.

Blake Fenway and Caroline sat together, hand in hand, on the little sofa to the right of the fire; Craddock stood dejected at the other end of the hearth, his elbow on the mantel, his head bent, his eyes on the flames. Gamadge had effaced himself in the bay window, where he leant with his arms on the glassy top of the old Steinway. Nordhall faced them all from his position just within the door from the reception room.

"I just want to say it again before Mr. Fenway," said Craddock. "What I said before, Lieutenant; it's all my fault."

Fenway raised his head to look at him. "Yours, my boy?"

"Yes, sir. I bought him a toy pistol and showed him how to pull the trigger. You understand? If it hadn't been for me he wouldn't have known how to kill the woman. He would only have taken the gun away from her. He was imitating what she had done, but if I hadn't explained the thing to him he wouldn't have known how. He wouldn't have hit her at all if he hadn't jammed the thing up against her forehead."

Caroline said in a low voice: "Must we hear it all over again?" and Craddock straightened to look at her sternly.

"I'm thinking of him," he said. "His future's more important to me than other peoples' feelings just now, Miss Fenway."

Blake Fenway said: "Craddock."

"I know, sir. I'm behaving badly; but it may

make all the difference to Alden if the police understand that he never was violent in his life before, and most probably never will be again. It isn't in him. Why, if you or I had done what he did somebody'd want to give us a medal; but because he's got the brain of a child he'll suffer for acting like a man."

Nordhall's eyes showed appreciation of this point. He said: "Something in what you say, but the trouble is — and let me tell you Thurley himself agrees with me — Alden Fenway's proved he can commit an act of violence, and whether it's just or unjust to reason that way, I think it's pretty well proven that he'll be better from now on in a place where they understand his kind of case. I'm all for institutional care in these cases myself. I think the patient's better off, and I think the relatives are. I'm afraid Mrs. Fenway may put up a fight for it, she's wrapped up in him, but I thought I'd just suggest that I don't think she'll win out. Of course if the family backs her —"

Caroline said: "There's only my father."

Blake Fenway put his hand up to his eyes. He said: "I see Craddock's point of view."

"Father —" Caroline turned to face him. "Yes, my dear?"

"Aunt Belle didn't say anything about the picture of Fenbrook, did she?"

He dropped his hand from his face to look at her in astonishment. "The picture of Fenbrook?"

"Mrs. Grove doesn't seem to have done *that*, does she?"

"Done what?"

"Torn it out."

"Mrs. Grove? Why should she tear it out?"

"There doesn't seem to be any reason why; and Cousin Mott and I thought Alden did."

Nordhall said with what seemed only mild interest, "What picture was that, Miss Fenway?"

"A picture of our old house; it was torn out of a book that was sent to us here from Fenbrook a week ago Thursday, and that's when all the trouble seems to have started. Aunt Belle says that Mrs. Grove began to blackmail her then, doesn't she?"

"Yes."

Fenway said: "We don't know when the picture was torn out, Caroline."

"No, but you found that it was gone on Friday evening, and Cousin Mott and I were sure Alden did it. We thought he was changing — turning mischievous and destructive. Father, we were so afraid of Alden — I mean I was — that I thought *he* killed Cousin Mott last night."

Craddock shouted out: "What do you

mean?" But Nordhall's eye quelled him. He said: "You don't think so now, Miss Fenway, do you?"

"No, but —"

Craddock spoke again, but quietly and with repressed feeling: "The idea's ridiculous. We all know why he killed Mrs. Grove, though of course he didn't know he was killing her, he doesn't know the meaning of the word. He's not vicious. I think it's a crime to accuse *him* of a deliberate crime without evidence."

Nordhall shook his head. "Miss Fenway's just saying she wants her cousin out of the house because he got on her nerves — and she says he got on Mr. Mott Fenway's nerves. She's not exactly accusing him of anything. No evidence, Miss Fenway?"

"No."

"Well, I'll tell you what we think of doing now. We're going to take the young fellow to a hospital for observation, Thurley will make arrangements; take him tonight. He'll have all the comforts you want to provide him with, and there won't be any question so far as I know of anything like a trial or anything like that. But I wouldn't count on his being let loose again; I don't think that's on the cards. No question of jail. Craddock here can go along with him tonight, and when Mrs. Fenway gets better she can be with him as much as she wants to. If you'll coöperate — explain to her —"

Craddock said: "I'll go along. You won't have any trouble with him, you know."

"We want to make things easy for you," continued Nordhall. "You've had a tough time of it, all because this Grove woman went out of her mind. I suppose she was one of these quiet, repressed characters that fly off the handle in the end?"

Fenway groaned. "You don't know how incredible the thing seems to us, Lieutenant; she wasn't a paid companion from an agency, you know; she was one of my sister-in-law's oldest friends."

"Yes. About this girl, now; this niece."

"Her husband's niece, Nordhall, and a really charming young girl. She ought to be here very soon now; she's on her way down, as I told you."

Craddock said between his teeth: "I don't believe in any trap at Fenbrook. Even that woman wasn't capable of such a thing."

"I'll have to stay and talk to her, of course." Nordhall's eye rested on him thoughtfully.

"She'll be in no state — she was fond of the woman!"

"Craddock," said Blake Fenway, "I can take care of Hilda Grove."

"And so can I," said Caroline. At the ex-

257

pression on Craddock's face she went on quietly: "And I will. She'll be here with us now. I don't know whether there's a trap at Fenbrook or whether there isn't, but she's been alone there long enough. It makes me sick to think of it — to think that that woman could even have imagined such a thing against her. She's thoroughly nice, Lieutenant Nordhall, and I wish you didn't have to say a word to her tonight."

"She's been up there for some time?"

"She hasn't seen Mrs. Grove for more than five weeks."

"Then she wouldn't have noticed anything funny about her. Wouldn't be much help to us." Lieutenant Nordhall's considerateness was phenomenal. "I may not even talk to her."

At that moment the doorbell rang, and shortly afterwards a policeman came in to say that a Sergeant Bantz, describing himself as assistant to Mr. Henry Gamadge, wanted to speak to Mr. Gamadge.

"Sergeant of what?" inquired Nordhall.

"Of Marines. If I might take him into the library?" Gamadge rose. "Probably he has some business message."

Blake Fenway said of course, Nordhall made no objection, and Gamadge went out of the room. The doorbell rang again, and this time the officer announced Miss Grove.

Arline Prady, having seen her into the house, gracefully retired without waiting for an invitation to stay. The occupants of the back drawing room surged into the hall, and Hilda, in tears, flung herself upon Mr. William Craddock. It was in the arms of her oldest friend that she responded to Blake Fenway's gentle words of sympathy; then Caroline took charge of her and persuaded her upstairs; she was to have her old room on the top floor, but Caroline was to be in Mott Fenway's room that night, and Craddock — he explained a dozen times as he followed them — would be a few yards away.

Gamadge did not emerge from the library with Harold until Hilda had left the first floor; he had no wish to be recognized with surprise as Mr. Hendrix. He ushered Harold out into the night, and turned to find Lieutenant Nordhall at his elbow. The Lieutenant still wore his expression of cool detachment and calm authority, but something had been added to it — an enquiring and a slightly puzzled look; a look, in fact, which Gamadge was used to seeing on the faces of policemen.

"You're *that* Gamadge," he said.

"Am I?"

"Mr. Fenway was just telling me. Would you oblige me by stepping back to the library?"

"I was waiting to ask you to do that."

"And I was waiting to see that you didn't go off with your assistant." The lieutenant went ahead of Gamadge down the now deserted hall. He waited for Gamadge to pass him into the library, closed the door, and then looked out of the other one. When he had shut it too, he turned to see Gamadge looking at him with a mirthless half-smile.

"What's funny?" he asked, raising a pale eyebrow.

"Nothing's funny. I was again comparing the methods of the amateur and the pro."

"If you're an amateur I'm another. How about sitting down and having a little talk — just to review the case before we close it up. We're all being so nice and frank, Miss Fenway and all, I thought it wouldn't hurt if you should take it into your head to be nice and frank with me."

"It won't hurt me, Lieutenant."

"Fine."

They sat down opposite each other in front of the now dying embers of the fire. They offered each other cigarette cases, politely shook their heads, and lighted up independently.

"What I mean to suggest is," said Nordhall, "that you haven't the reputation of being the kind of man that walks in on tragedies by accident."

Gamadge was leaning back in his deep chair, knees crossed, his cigarette sending up a quivering spiral of blue that mushroomed into gray; he seemed inattentive to Nordhall's words; his eyes were partly shut, his look withdrawn. He murmured something.

"Last night," continued Nordhall, "I didn't know who you were; I didn't know that yesterday was the first time you'd ever been inside the house or met the family. I didn't know you came here because some relation of yours wrote and asked Mr. Fenway to ask you to come. I heard all this because I asked Mr. Fenway about you just now, and I asked him about you because I finally realized that he didn't know how you came to be on the spot two hours ago."

"I brought some books."

"The day after a death in the house you brought some books; only it wasn't a death in the house, it was a violent death out of a window, and you'd met the family the day before for the first time. When I found you here today I thought you must have been brought up with Miss Fenway, or something."

"Didn't she explain that I'd been calling on her?" Gamadge turned half-shut eyes on the other, and faintly smiled at him.

261

"Yes, she did her best for you; but she couldn't explain how you came to be wandering round in the upper hall alone, and how you managed to overhear those bits of conversation before the door was slammed in your face and locked. If it hadn't been, you'd have prevented the fatality."

"Or been shot myself." Gamadge sat up and looked at Nordhall through open eyes. "I could make up some story; I could say I'd gone back to say something or find something; but I haven't the least desire to make up a story. I want to talk to you as frankly as you please, but I must admit that I should have liked to find something first."

"Find what?"

"That picture you heard about; the one that was torn out of Mr. Fenway's book of views."

"The one Miss Fenway says Alden tore out? I don't believe he did it."

"Neither do I."

"Nobody with the brain of a child would take any interest in a place he never saw and wouldn't remember hearing about. And if he was only looking through the book as if it was a picture book, it's too much of a coincidence for him to spoil that particular page by accident."

"Much too much."

"Miss Fenway seems bound to get him into

an asylum." Nordhall looked at Gamadge sharply. "In that case what becomes of his property?"

"I don't know how it would be administered, but Caroline Fenway would have no rights in her cousin Alden's money, during his life or after his death. It would go to his mother if he died."

"Nothing in that, then. And he's safe with that mother of his; she'd starve to death for him."

"I really think she would."

"That being the case, why do you want to find the picture? And what's it got to do with you getting yourself into this house yesterday and today? What made you expect trouble, that's the thing I'd like to know."

"I was tipped off."

"By Mott Fenway?"

"Mott Fenway didn't ask me to come to the house on Sunday afternoon; he spoke to me as I was leaving yesterday; suggested that I should come back last night and look for the lost picture. His theory was the same as Miss Fenway's, you know."

"And why didn't you mention the fact last night — that he was killed before you could get here?"

"I had no evidence that he was killed because he was going to let me in secretly."

Nordhall said with his coldest look: "I guess you are an amateur, after all. If you'd seen fit to give me this information at the time I would have asked some more questions, and I would have broken down Mrs. Grove's alibi."

"Would you?"

"I would have seen the parties alone and separate, and Mrs. Fenway would have told me all about the blackmail. Now Mrs. Grove has been shot dead instead of standing trial for Mott Fenway's murder, and Alden Fenway will go to a private asylum for life — unless they get tough and send him to Matteawan — and his mother's about ready to qualify for Bloomingdale herself. That's what you get for poking around looking for evidence on your own. Or were you?"

"Well, yes, I was; and I have some. I hope for more, if you —"

"Just let me get this out of you my way, if you don't mind. When were you tipped off first, and who tipped you?"

"I was tipped off on Saturday," said Gamadge mildly, "by what you might call an anonymous letter."

"Sent by Mott Fenway, of course; unless Caroline Fenway sent it without telling him."

"Or," continued Gamadge, politely ignoring this, "you might call it a code message.

The details of it won't matter to you now —"

"Oh; won't they?" Nordhall had so far relaxed his Olympian calm as to condescend to sarcasm.

"No, but you can have all the details later if you want them. I really don't think you will want them. I had reason to think that the sender of this letter or message had been trying to reach me for more than a week; ever since the day when — as I personally believe — that picture was torn out of the book of views.

"The message was cryptic, but it seemed to ask me to investigate conditions in this house. I got myself invited here, you're quite right about it; and the first thing I found that could be considered at all out of the way was the fact that that picture of Fenbrook was lost, and that the discovery of the loss had been made the day the first anonymous message was sent to me."

Nordhall was now sitting forward on the edge of his chair, his mouth slightly open and his hands on his knees; but he said nothing.

"The next thing I found here," continued Gamadge, "was a second message, or what seemed like one; I found it in a wastebasket in the sitting room. It seemed to suggest a trip to Fenbrook, so I went up there with my assistant yesterday afternoon. I met Hilda Grove, and I decided to leave Bantz in the neighborhood. I returned here to find Mott Fenway dead; but I also found a third message, which I interpreted as best I could. I thought it meant that somebody or something must be removed from Fenbrook."

Nordhall could contain himself no longer: "What did it *say?*"

"It didn't say a thing. It was a timetable, a Rockliffe timetable, with an arrow pointing nowhere. Away from Rockliffe, I mean."

Nordhall slowly sat back, his eyes on Gamadge, his hands sliding along his pin-striped blue trousers.

"My assistant agreeing with my conclusions," continued Gamadge, "he took Miss Hilda Grove temporarily out of Fenbrook. The pretext was a coasting party, and he assured me when he was here a little while ago that that coasting party was not the least of many hazards which he has survived during the past year.

"Pursuing my instructions, he afterwards searched Fenbrook for a concealed peril or a trap."

"You knew there was a trap?"

"I imagined a trap," said Gamadge modestly.

"That's more than I did. I don't believe

there was a trap. Bantz didn't find one, I suppose?"

"He found one; a disused dumb-waiter shaft, which had at some time been converted into a tier of corner cupboards by means of removable floorings. Bantz found that the floorings had been removed. In the attic cupboard he found Mrs. Grove's knitting bag on an innermost hook, out of reach unless he stepped in. If he were not the most skeptical and cautious of human beings he would have stepped in, and would now probably be lying dead on the cement floor of the disused basement-kitchen."

Nordhall's light eyes were like marbles. "That cupboard was there for anybody to step into?"

"No, it was locked. But Bantz found the key in the attic; Hilda Grove would have found it easily enough if somebody telephoned instructions to her. I may add that Bantz and I were particularly interested in the attic because Hilda Grove heard somebody there on the night of the twenty-first. That," said Gamadge, mildly regarding Nordhall, "was the day the book of views came to this house, and the day — as I suppose — that the first anonymous message was sent out of this house to me."

"That little scrap of a woman went up there

267

in the middle of the night!"

"You don't perhaps know what the climb from Rockliffe Station is like. Harold and I did it yesterday."

"They say crazy people can do things they couldn't do if they were sane, and now I believe it. Mrs. Fenway is right; that woman had been driven out of her mind by the war and her troubles, and I'm not so sure I'm sorry she's dead."

"Humane of you, very humane."

Nordhall suddenly got to his feet. "Did Bantz put back those floors or anything?"

"Oh, no; he left things as they were, of course; but of course he relocked the cupboard door."

"And one of those locals I had them send up to the place will bust it open and walk in. Where's the nearest telephone?"

But Nordhall knew where it was; in the stress of the moment he had forgotten. He strode towards the door to the back passage, then stopped. "Fenway didn't get any answer when he called up this evening. Wires may be down."

"I think you'll find that you can reach Fenbrook now."

Nordhall, with a dark look at his colleague, vanished. After a few minutes, he came back and sank into chair. "They were looking for time bombs in the cellar," he muttered.

"Harold was quite prepared to find an infernal machine. And now, that being off our minds, don't you think, Nordhall, that we might have a look for the lost picture of Fenbrook?"

"How the dickens does it tie up with the case? I think it's only a coincidence," said Nordhall with some irritation. "I know what you think — that it's being lost started all the trouble. But if so, Mrs. Fenway doesn't know it, she hasn't said a word about it. And it doesn't matter now whether Alden Fenway tore it out or not."

"He didn't tear it out."

"Well, then? Why the hurry?"

"I'd better show you the book of views." Gamadge went across the room, got the green velvet quarto out of the inlaid coffer, and returned to lay it open on the broad arm of Nordhall's chair.

"That's where the view of Fenbrook was," he said.

18

LOST VIEW

"It was taken out nicely, all right," said Nordhall. "Kind of a horrible mutilation, though. Who's this Julian Fenway that wrote the piece about it? Grandfather? I don't blame the family for not wanting to lose the picture of the house."

"If you'll turn to the Delabar King plate, and the Colonel Ash one, you'll find incised marks on them and on the tissue guards. You won't make much of them without a reading glass," said Gamadge, "and there's a reading glass on Blake Fenway's desk. While you were telephoning I convinced myself that it's a well-equipped library. However, you may be willing to take my word for it that there's part of a facsimile of Cort Fenway's signature on one of the pictures and on its guard."

"Cort Fenway? Wasn't he the Fenway brother that died twenty years ago — Mrs. Fenway's husband?"

"Yes. He made those marks soon before he died, I think; made them because he used the book as a writing pad. My idea is that we'll find more and clearer traces of his writing on the lost view."

"Oh. Now I get it." Nordhall's face changed. "Blackmail? But Mrs. Fenway wasn't being blackmailed with the picture, or if she was she hasn't said so."

"She wasn't."

"You seem to know a lot about it." Nordhall again turned a grim appraising look on his ally. "Was Mrs. Grove going to blackmail *Fenway?*"

"I should know more about it if we found it."

"Find it in a house of this size?" Nordhall's tone was pitying. "It would take a couple of trained men a week. It could be rolled up and stuffed into a pipe, or folded and put into any of these thousands of books." His eyes wandered over the towering shelves.

"It wasn't rolled or folded; the marks on it had to be preserved in good condition, not broken or obscured by rubbing and creasing. And if it wasn't folded it couldn't have been put into any book smaller than a quarto, which eliminates three-quarters of the volumes in this library."

"It could be under a carpet; a nailed carpet."

"Fingers couldn't push it farther than fingers could reach it. You don't understand,

271

Nordhall; this was hidden so that it shouldn't be found, even by a free and most intensive search. It's been searched for, you know; Fenway has had it searched for since the twenty-second of January, and I'm sure that Mott Fenway and Caroline had a good look for it too, not to mention others."

"It could be buried in the garden in a waterproof case, or locked up in a safe-deposit box."

"I don't think it was taken out of this room."

"You don't?"

"No. Tell you why later."

Nordhall again glanced up at the bookshelves in front of him. "What about sliding it down behind the books on a shelf?"

"It would be seen at a glance by anyone who chose to get up on those library steps there, and pull out two or three volumes from each section."

"It wouldn't be seen at a glance if it was in any of those big books, and there are plenty."

"I don't like to contradict you, but it would; it's on the stiffest of fine thick paper, and would be noticed instantly."

"I suppose it wouldn't be on top of these high cases, or that cabinet?"

"Servants dust the tops of things."

Nordhall flung himself back in his chair. "You tell me all about it."

"I'll tell you what I think went on in this library in the late afternoon of Thursday, January the twenty-first; perhaps on the following morning, but somehow I think it happened on Thursday afternoon. The books came down, Mr. Fenway unwrapped them, and they lay accessible on that long table in the bay window on your right. Fenway didn't examine the consignment — he hadn't the time. Mrs. Grove wandered in, and was interested in the lot which her niece had just sent down; she was particularly interested in the set of *Views On The Hudson,* probably because Fenway had been talking about it. She had never had her attention called to it at Fenbrook. She wasn't a Fenway, you know, and Mrs. Fenway wasn't either; she might never have heard of old Fenbrook until recently.

"Now she looked for the picture of it; she found it, and on it she found incised markings, which she deciphered by means of that reading glass I spoke of. I won't try to describe how she looked when she did decipher them, because until we decipher them ourselves we shan't be able to guess how profound her emotions were. But when she had recovered herself she must have hunted feverishly through the book for other markings; she realized, of course, exactly what had happened and what Cort Fenway had unconsciously done. The other marks were innocuous, so she left them; and since she couldn't easily hide the book, she tore out the picture and its tissue guard.

"What to do with them? She must have looked about her wildly, thinking that if she could find a hiding place for them in the library she would not have to run the risk of carrying them upstairs; she would leave no clue to their hiding place at all. And she realized other facts; that a library is equipped with other things as useful at a pinch as a reading glass, and that servants don't dust the undersides of things."

"They don't?" Nordhall shifted his legs. "They tip up chairs and tables." He looked at the highboy opposite, and at Gamadge. "You don't mean . . . ?"

Gamadge, smiling, shook his head. "I tried."

"You thought it would be stuck —"

"Mrs. Grove wished to preserve it carefully; and there's paste in the desk, Nordhall, library paste, and large Manila envelopes."

"You've found it!"

"No; I waited for you. What in this room can be lifted but not tipped? What is there that we couldn't shove our hands under?"

Nordhall gazed about him; then he rose and

followed Gamadge to the buhl table.

"Give me a hand," said Gamadge, his fingers under one end of the inlaid coffer. "This thing weighs a lot — it's ivory on old brass; and servants wouldn't be allowed to shove it around on that buhl, and if it's tipped the lid will fall open. It doesn't clear the table by more than an inch, and if it's ever moved at all, which I doubt —" they had raised the coffer, to disclose a thick layer of dust — "it's lifted as we're lifting it now."

They moved the thing to the edge of a solid table, where Gamadge balanced it while Nordhall bent to peer upwards. He gave an exclamation, and ripped something from beneath the coffer. When he rose he held in his fingers a large Manila envelope smeared in patches with dried paste.

"Neat," said Gamadge. "She could just get her fingers under far enough to hold the envelope against the brass till it stuck. Very neat. A most intelligent woman."

Nordhall gazed at him. "Why did you think it was here?"

"Well, there didn't seem to be much reason for it to be anywhere else. Let's see old Fenbrook."

Nordhall drew a picture from the envelope; a delicately colored view of a white house on a hill, surrounded by trees. A thin leaf of tissue fluttered after it, to be caught on Gamadge's open hand. Nordhall took it from him; then he laid the thick leaf and the thin aside, and helped Gamadge to replace the inlaid casket.

He turned on a reading lamp, got the magnifying glass from the desk, and put the two sheets side by side. Gamadge watched while he stood bent and peering. Suddenly he cried aloud: "For God's sake."

Gamadge said nothing; hands in pockets, he waited.

Nordhall again studied and compared the picture and its guard. When he at last stood up straight his whole body was tense, the lines of his face rigid. He handed the reading glass to Gamadge, and waited. Gamadge bent to the exhibits on the table. When he in turn straightened, Nordhall spoke sharply: "You expected this."

"Something like it."

"That poor woman upstairs sent you the anonymous messages."

"Yes. I'll tell you the whole story — afterwards."

"Take care of that." Nordhall gestured violently at the evidence, and plunged across the room. He dragged the door open, left it open, and disappeared into the hall. He could be heard thundering up the stairs.

Gamadge stood in an attitude of listening,

his face raised. He heard voices, a sudden sound of trampling, a shout like a warning. It was answered by the flat, muffled noise of a pistol shot. Gamadge relaxed against the edge of the table; he was smiling.

Presently Blake Fenway appeared in the doorway. He said: "There's a policeman on the stairs with a gun in his hand; he says I'm not to go up. He won't tell me who was shot, or what's happened. Do you understand this?" His face had altered; it resembled that of the portrait over the mantel, even to the severity of the mouth and eyes.

Gamadge said: "I think I know pretty much what occurred upstairs, Mr. Fenway, and why it occurred." He pointed to the view of Fenbrook. "I found your picture."

"My picture?" Fenway did not seem to know what he meant. Then, glancing at it, he said in a voice of sudden bewilderment: "What has the picture to do with all this?"

"Will you look at it, sir?"

Fenway came slowly across the room to look down at his picture; he said almost with indifference: "There are marks on it."

"They are the tracings of your brother's pencil."

"My brother's . . . what do you mean?"

"Mr. Cort Fenway wrote a letter on thin

paper, and the marks of his pencil came through. You can read what he wrote through your glass."

He offered the glass to Fenway; but Fenway shook his head. "You've read it?" he asked.

"I have read it, and Nordhall has read it."

"Then tell me what it says."

"You wouldn't rather look at it first yourself?"

"Why should I? It is no longer a private document."

"It's not a document at all, sir, in the accepted sense of the word. It's the impression of a document, graven indelibly on these two sheets of paper, and signed with your brother's signature. There are other such impressions in the book of views, also signed by him, but they're fragmentary. This is practically whole."

"If — as you seem to suggest — it alleges anything against my brother, it's a forgery."

Gamadge looked at the other in surprise. "Against him? It's much to his credit; it bears out all that I've heard or gathered about your brother. I'll read it to you, Mr. Fenway, but only if you'll sit down to listen."

Fenway went over to the fire and sank into his chair. Gamadge could not see his face; he read:

"My dearest Belle,

Since as you tell me our poor little Alden cannot live, we must certainly adopt your boy. I am glad to think that you will be comforted by having a child of your own still with you, and that he is so near you now.

You know how much impressed I was, the last time I saw him, by his intelligence and health and good looks. I shall be more than happy to have him as one of the family. We can arrange the adoption without the slightest risk to you; it will seem natural enough for us to do it.

I have, as you asked, said nothing here about Alden's hopeless condition, and shall say nothing until you give me leave. I understand that you want to be alone with me in this sorrow.

I shall be with you very soon.

Cort."

There was absolute silence in the library. When at last Gamadge reluctantly and slowly raised his eyes, he saw that Fenway had turned his head and was looking at him. "Does it mean," asked a voice that was Fenway's and yet not his own, "that that — young man upstairs —"

"He is nothing to you, sir."

"Then he's not — if he's not Alden, he's sane."

"Yes."

"Belle has been cheating us all these years." After a pause he added: "And her son has been malingering all his life."

"I dare say he never had much occasion to play his part until the voyage home, after he and his mother met Mrs. Grove. I suppose all the talk of specialists and sanatoria in Europe was pure invention; we can't check up on them, you know. And he's never had tests made by specialists here, has he? Wasn't he protected from them by Thurley, who never doubted him at all? Why should he have doubted him? That's why they stayed with you, you know; to avoid the draft tests and enquiries. Thurley would protect him there."

"Caroline was afraid of him."

"She must have seen him off guard once or twice, and realized unconsciously that he was sane."

"In God's name why did they do it?"

Gamadge, looking down at the view of Fenbrook, asked a question in his turn: "What was to become of that half of the Fenway property if your brother died childless?"

Fenway twisted in his chair to look at the questioner. Gamadge came and sat opposite him.

Fenway said: "It returned to the estate; it would eventually go to Caroline."

"So I thought, from what little I heard about it. I think Alden died before your brother did, Mr. Fenway."

"What!"

"He died in this country; Alden was alone with his mother abroad."

"The villa was isolated, and her servants didn't sleep on the place. Cort was anxious about her, but she liked to be free of them at night. She was fearless, fearless."

"Did you cable her when he was taken ill?"

"Immediately."

"She made plans then; she saw how she could retain the fortune for herself and her own son. I suppose he can't be much older than Alden would have been if he had lived, two or three years. There wasn't any rumor or scandal about her, I suppose?"

"No, or my father and mother wouldn't have allowed the marriage." He added: "I mean they wouldn't have financed it. She was very lively and gay, and her mother would have concealed anything; got her to Europe in spite of the other war. Cort was there of course, almost from the first; as a volunteer in France, and then with our army. He would have helped her — it was like him. Yes; that romantic marriage was protection for her; and of course my brother would befriend her boy."

"Allow her her virtues," said Gamadge. "If your brother loved her, she loved her eldest son — passionately."

"Is that virtue?" Fenway's voice was dry. He went on: "What kind of creature can he be? How can he have carried on such a deception, day and night? I should think he would have gone mad."

"I think he lived his own life at night, Mr. Fenway. I think he was often out of this house, and that when your daughter brought her dog here he killed it, so that it wouldn't bark when he went and came."

"Monstrous!"

"And when the draft menace was over, he and his mother would have gone away together, and he would have dropped his mask. They would have worked out some arrangement by which he might safely have drawn his income after her death. Keep your mind on that income, Mr. Fenway; it was worth everything to them, worth a lot of risk."

Fenway suddenly looked up. "Mrs. Grove . . ."

"With Mrs. Grove we arrive at tragedy. Last Thursday afternoon she was in this library, she was interested in the last consignment which her niece had sent down from

Fenbrook; the poor woman was very much interested indeed in the book of views, in all things pertaining to you and your family. She found the picture of old Fenbrook; no doubt she had heard of it from you. She found those marks on it, deciphered them, and went directly upstairs to Mrs. Fenway. She insisted on full confession of the conspiracy to you, which meant the loss of what they had risked so much to keep; half the Fenway fortune. She acted without due thought; she couldn't realize in a moment that the old friend over whom she had once had so much influence, that the young man who had long been to her a nonentity, would commit murder. She confronted two tigers.

"They have been looking for the picture; meanwhile, they have been keeping her as much a prisoner as if she had been in a condemned cell. She was in one; she could only have escaped alive by confiding fully in me. She wouldn't; do you know why?"

Fenway shook his head.

"Sublime folly! She wouldn't confide this family secret to anyone but you; her devotion to you and yours cost her her life. But I was wrong a moment ago; she might have saved it this afternoon if she had waited to speak until you were actually there. She didn't know that they had a prearranged plan for an emergency. The moment they knew that she was going to speak they killed her, and the fellow shot his mother through the arm. I'm sure they'd rehearsed it."

After a pause Fenway spoke slowly: "I liked her. Caroline didn't, but I always liked her."

"Her loyalty to you was absolute, and her affection for her niece Hilda was very great. If it hadn't been, those two couldn't have kept her helpless and silent by telling her that there was a trap at Fenbrook."

"There actually is one?"

"There is one, and it was not made only to frighten her; it would have been used as evidence against her after her death. It was the fear of the trap that made her call me in, God help her."

"Called you in?"

"By means of a scrap of paper thrown out of a window. The message was vague — it had to be. Imagine her position, hemmed in by those two desperate creatures; and she had nearly two weeks of it! But they couldn't budge her, and she couldn't move until I was able to tell her that I had read her instructions correctly and removed Hilda from Fenbrook. Then she acted — half a minute too soon; and then *they* acted — as they had planned to act if worst came to worst. They could do nothing else; they had to let the picture go;

they hoped that if they hadn't been able to find it it wouldn't be found."

Fenway asked: "They meant to kill her even if she gave up the picture to them?"

"I don't doubt it. They didn't hesitate to kill Mr. Mott Fenway."

"They killed Mott!"

"Because he had invited me to come here and look for the lost view. He was against them, and they were afraid of him."

Fenway's hand clenched. Gamadge went on: "Your house has been haunted by a sane, intelligent, ruthless man and a woman who would have died for him. Mrs. Grove stood like a rock between them and the ultimate success of the most cynical and heartless imposture I ever heard of. She has accomplished her purpose, and I don't think she would have grudged the cost to herself. And I tried as best I could to help her accomplish that purpose; for I didn't look for the picture, and invade the Fenway privacy —" he smiled a little — "until she was no longer able to expose the conspiracy. But I wish she had let me save her."

"Great Heaven, if she only had!"

"There must be something that inspires devotion in you Fenways, sir."

"If you had only warned us that something was wrong!"

"I couldn't for two reasons: I didn't know what the cost might be to my client — her instructions were as I said very vague; and I had no evidence."

"No evidence?"

"Against your sister-in-law and her eldest son? No. The evidence," said Gamadge, pointing to the view of Fenbrook, "is there. It's all Mrs. Grove had, and Nordhall and I first saw it twenty minutes ago."

"Nordhall . . ." Fenway got to his feet. "Where is he? What did he do?"

"I don't think you'll go through the agony of your sister-in-law's arrest and trial, Mr. Fenway. They didn't search *her* for a pistol, I suppose."

"What do you mean?"

"That shot we heard sounded like the other ones — sounded as if it came from one of those little guns. I imagine she had a pair of them, and that when he shouted to her that it was all up with him she used the other one on herself. Do you think she'd live if he couldn't?"

19

MR. BARGRAVE

Nordhall came into the room quietly; he had regained all his calm, and his manner was that of one who brings grave tidings. He said: "I don't know whether you'll think it's bad news or not, Mr. Fenway, or whether it's news at all; perhaps Mr. Gamadge guessed and told you."

Fenway spoke with frozen courtesy. He was like a man half stunned, or in a dream: "That my sister-in-law is dead?"

"She's dead. The minute I told that fellow that we'd found a letter on that picture there, he shoved open the door of his room and shouted out to her that it was all over. She must have had the other little gun in the pocket of her robe all the time. She was lying on top of the bed — hadn't let the nurse undress her or give her a sedative; she was waiting to make sure everything was all right, that they'd got away with murder. She pulled the gun out and shot herself."

After a moment Fenway spoke in a louder

voice: "Where is Caroline?"

"All right; up on the top floor with Miss Grove. We wouldn't let them come down. Craddock came — ran half way and then jumped the banisters; but he pulled up short when he saw that fellow — the imposter — I can tell you! Quite a shock for him. But he has Miss Grove to think of. He's with her now. That's a nice little lady," said Nordhall, an eye on Fenway's expressionless face. "Nice pair they make. Craddock says they're going to be together from now on, even if they starve to death; till they pass him for the war, of course. The little lady say's so too."

Fenway seemed to come to life at that; he slightly shook his head. "Starve? Craddock must be raving. They won't starve. I shall make Hilda my responsibility until he can take care of her."

Nordhall, pleased with his tactics, went on: "I'm glad we didn't tell her anything about her aunt being suspected of blackmail and the rest of it. Touch and go, wasn't it? You know, when I saw those marks on that picture, read that letter, the whole thing shifted around in my head like one of those things we used to have in the parlor — what do you call them? Kaleidoscopes. Pattern shifted around in my head. I'll tell you something, Mr. Fenway; this has turned out better for you than you realize now. I know it's tough now, but at least you won't have to see your brother's wife in court convicted of fraud and conspiracy, and probably of being accessory to murder. Of course that fellow may swear it was all his own idea, and that he coerced her by threats."

Gamadge moved a shoulder. "She wouldn't have let him swear to that."

"The point is," continued Nordhall, "that just now he's ready to say anything. He wants to talk to you, Mr. Fenway."

Fenway raised a blank face. "Now?"

"I know how you feel, sir, nobody on earth you'd less rather see. Eerie, too; you won't know him. Craddock was knocked silly for a minute. But you're prepared, and to tell you the truth you'll be doing us a great favor. He may not talk again. He's a feller that does what he starts out to do, and just now he's all keyed up to tell you the whole thing. The statement will be a voluntary statement, you and Mr. Gamadge will be witnesses, it will clear up a lot of things you'd like to know yourself, and I've got a stenographer."

There was a long silence. Then Fenway, leaning back in his chair and averting his face, said in a low voice: "I'll see him."

"Thanks very much. People like you can be depended on, Mr. Fenway, and that's a fact." Nordhall turned to the doorway and jerked his head. A uniformed man moved out of sight, and then returned.

Presently two persons came in, walking side by side and close together; two persons who at first glance seemed to Gamadge to be strangers; but only one of them — the plain-clothes man — was a stranger; the other, a tall, broad-shouldered, good-looking fellow with an air of competence and alertness about him, was Mrs. Cort Fenway's eldest son without his mask.

"Thanks very much for seeing me, sir," he rapped out in a staccato and businesslike way; and his voice was a stranger's voice too. "I can imagine what an effort it must be for you, but I know you'll appreciate my position. I simply want to do my mother justice."

Fenway slowly turned in his chair to face him, and sat regarding him with a kind of shocked incredulity; as if he were a fabulous monster turned real. Gamadge, studying the blond giant with interest, had the curious impression that in regaining his own personality the impostor had lost half his breeding. He had been far more like a Fenway before; now, having dropped the disguise, he exposed himself as a type that used to be seen swaggering in the casinos and at the race-meetings of Europe — coarse-grained, arrogant and knowing.

He glanced from Fenway's bleak face to Gamadge's, and favored the latter with a half-smile. "How did she get the S.O.S. to you?" he asked curiously.

The plain-clothes man slightly jerked his wrist, which — as could now be seen — was riveted to the impostor's with steel. The prisoner looked down at his gyved hand, and put it in his pocket. "All right," he said. "I suppose I won't be allowed even to ask you where that damned picture was."

Gamadge moved his head to the right; the other followed the motion like a flash, and Gamadge said: "Pasted under the coffer."

"Well, I'll be — I've been looking for it every night since a week ago Thursday, when that woman came and told us — but that's over. Still, when you think how much depended on it, you'd suppose I ought to have turned the trick. Too nervous, perhaps, with a houseful of people above and below. Well."

He paused, took countenance, and faced Blake Fenway again.

"I'd like to say first," he went on briskly, "that you mustn't be shocked at my attitude; it isn't frivolous. My mother brought me up to regard it all as a gamble, and I knew what she'd do if we lost. I was prepared, and I'm glad she's out of it. Mind you, the only reason we did lose was because the war came, and she got hurt on that cursed boat, and had to have somebody to take care of her. And of course I had to impersonate Alden Fenway in this house, or be had up before a draft board and all kinds of intelligence tests.

"The impersonation wasn't as hard as you'd think. I was coached young. I mean we had a look round at cases in the big institutions in Europe, and my mother asked plenty of questions. Then we'd practice at pensions and hotels, and really there wasn't much to it. Here in this house I only had to keep it up from late breakfast to early bedtime, and after that I could lead my own life and have some fun."

Gamadge, leaning rather wearily against the side of the mantelpiece, looked up from the still wearier figure of his host to interrupt the speaker: "You found yourself under the sad necessity of killing Miss Fenway's dog, I think."

The alert blue eyes clouded. "Now I rather wish you hadn't brought that up. I was awfully sorry about that. Dangerous, too; but I managed somehow."

"Mr. Mott Fenway thought Craddock had done it."

"Mr. Mott Fenway had too many bright thoughts. Anyhow, I was able to lead almost as good a life as my mother and I led in Europe; we travelled, we let each other alone and had our own amusements. What a sport she was! It was hard on her here, being cooped up; but she didn't mind, except for worrying about me. She didn't dare move away from the family, of course, because we were afraid I'd be put through some of these modern tests for I.Q. — as I said. Neither of us knew what the scientific methods are now, and I don't have to tell you that we didn't consult specialists in Europe."

Gamadge said: "Not even Fagon in Paris."

At the other's laugh Fenway glanced up, then closed his eyes and let his head sink back against the cushions of his chair. "Fagon? Poor soul. We hoped his casebooks and his records *were* lost. We had to take a gamble on that. We were getting along all right, except for Caroline and Mott getting sick of us, and Mott watching me. And then along came that confounded book, and Mrs. Grove rushed up on Thursday afternoon to throw her bomb; that there was a signed letter traced through on a page — on the picture of old Fenbrook. She said it was from Cort Fenway to Mother, and that it proved I wasn't Alden. She said the Fenways had been done out of half their money, and that unless Mother confessed, she'd tell. Fuss about nothing; what harm had we done? The Fenways didn't want or need the money, and Cort Fenway would have liked me to have it. He liked *me* — he was going to adopt me. But that obstinate fool of a woman, who never acquired any knowledge of the world or any kind of broad views after she left boarding school — we couldn't make her see it." He glanced about him with a frown. "She was always burrowing in this room; I might have known she'd hide the picture here. I thought I'd pretty well covered the ground here, though. I was wasting time on the stair carpets."

Fenway opened his eyes to say tonelessly: "Belle ought to have known that I wouldn't prosecute."

"My dear, kind man, that wasn't the point; my mother was thinking of my interests — my income. Mrs. Grove didn't realize what she was up against; she never had a chance. But after Mott died she knew what she could expect if she persisted in trying to ruin us, and we didn't understand at the time why she kept going. I'm sorry about Mott, Mr. Fenway."

Fenway continued to stare at him.

"The thing is, I overheard Mott confiding in Gamadge yesterday. We couldn't have Gamadge looking for the picture; we were afraid that by some fluke he might find it — and damned if he didn't! So I acted on the spur of the moment and got rid of Mott, who seemed dangerous; but I oughtn't to have been so impulsive. He was a lot more dangerous to us dead than alive." The alert blue eyes turned to Gamadge. "You see why, don't you?"

Gamadge nodded, and the other went on, somewhat shamefacedly: "I was a fool. Hilda and the Dobsons would be invited to Mott's funeral; Mrs. Grove would know all about it, know they'd left Fenbrook, and burst out with her story as soon as she was sure they *had* left. You know about the trap; I fixed it up myself that same Thursday night, and a hell of a cold trip it was. We needed it to keep Mrs. Grove quiet, and we needed it for evidence against her if we finally had to put on the act we put on this afternoon. You know something, Gamadge? We never could have convinced her that the trap was there unless it really had been there. I realized that, when I was describing it to her. After that she couldn't keep her eyes off the telephone, and she never said another word about telling Fenway. Sly, wasn't she? I wish you'd tell me how she got the message through to you."

Gamadge said: "I rather hope you never will know that."

"Annoyed at losing your client after all, are you? Well, your client wasn't taking any chances with that telephone She knew that I could have reached it, or one of the others, before anybody could prevent me. I could tackle the whole crowd of them singlehanded, including Craddock."

He spoke with satisfaction. Gamadge murmured gently: "It *is* folie de grandeur," and was answered in a flash:

"No, it's not! There's nothing the matter with *my* brain."

Gamadge looked doubtful. "Such a life — it couldn't help but warp any human soul."

"Jargon! It was a wonderful life."

"I'm only trying to find some way of explaining you," said Gamadge, continuing to look at him as if in wonder.

"If you'll listen, you'll soon understand all about me and about my mother, too. Where was I? Oh yes; the shock we got this afternoon when we realized that Mrs. Grove was going to talk to Mr. Fenway after all; why, we couldn't imagine. We hadn't the faintest idea, of course, that Hilda had left Fenbrook — that you were on the job. Well, we went ahead with the scene we'd rehearsed in case of just such an emergency; and if Mother was upset afterwards you can't blame her — it's no joke to get a bullet in your arm, even if you're expecting it. Besides, we were a little flustered by your turning up outside the door, when we thought I had plenty of time to shut and lock it; time while Mr. Fenway came upstairs. But I did get it locked against you, and everything went off perfectly — our strategy of retreat. At least our part of it went off perfectly, and that's enough of that." He turned again to Blake Fenway. "What you're interested in, sir, is the substitution scheme, all those years ago. It's a very simple story.

"My mother and Alden were at the villa back of Cannes; peasant nursemaid with them, and a couple of servants that slept out. Cort Fenway had left for America. Alden had a turn for the worse, mentally and physically. Mother arranged for a specialist to come down from Paris, a visiting big shot from Russia; I may as well say now that he went to Sweden soon afterwards, and died there.

"He doomed Alden; growth on the brain, nothing to be done, matter of a few weeks. It had always been a possibility, it was part of the original diagnosis of Alden's case. Mother didn't say a word about it to her servants — she wasn't that sort; and it's lucky she wasn't, because she got word from America that Cort was seriously ill. You know what that meant to her — everything. If Alden died first, and Cort followed him, the Fenway money went back to the estate. She took no chances."

Blake Fenway's muffled voice interrupted him: "I would have taken care of her."

"But my mother wasn't sold on that idea, Mr. Fenway; an allowance from you might have kept her going, but she wanted more than that for me; she wanted what Alden would have come in for after his father died. For I was always in the offing; at that time I was boarded out with country people in the vicinity — she came to see me regularly, under an assumed name. And let me tell you that your brother sometimes came too!

"I don't believe anybody could honestly blame her for what she did. She was a general. She told the nursemaid that Alden needed trained care, had been ordered it by the specialist, and that he must be taken to Switzerland; she sent the girl home to her family in the north of France. When Alden died the other servants didn't know it; my mother buried him herself — in the grounds. Beautiful spot, she told me, under big trees. Anything so terrible about that?

"Then she left money for the servants and a letter and money for the agent; and a poste-restante address in Geneva. She said she was taking Alden to Switzerland, orders from the doctor. The villa was to be closed. Then she simply bundled herself and her traps into a car and came to me. She took me direct to a little place near Geneva, and drove in to the post office every day.

"When the cable arrived saying that Cort was dead, we went to Austria. There we stayed, travelling about, until I was old enough to pass as Alden. I was only three years and a little over, you know, and we both looked like her. You and Caroline met me for the first time in Paris when I was fifteen, Mr. Fenway; you may have thought me a little overgrown for my age, but you weren't unprepared to find me out of the ordinary, physically as well as mentally. No: we were perfectly safe. We didn't suppose that that Russian would ever hear of us or check up on us again, and he didn't; and by the time we were ready to go to Paris he was dead."

Gamadge asked mildly: "She had no trouble at all, even at first, with a child of your age — no trouble at all? You could keep such a secret even then, and learn to play such a part?"

"All I had to do for a long time was keep my mouth shut; and I was quite capable of doing that! It didn't take me long to realize the difference between a small income and a large one, I can tell you. Children are the greatest snobs in the world — next to dogs."

"If they're trained to be."

"Not much training required, my dear Mr.

Gamadge. And now, I really think that's all."
Mrs. Fenway's son, master of himself and —
so proudly did he bear himself — apparently
master of the situation, seemed about to turn
away; but Gamadge, hands in pockets and eyes
fixed on him in a kind of dark amusement,
said: "Well, no; not quite all. We don't even
now know who you are."

"Who I am?"

"Who you are. Or don't you care to say?"

"Of course I care to say. My father was
a thorough-going sport; I come by my ad-
venturous disposition from both sides of my
family. He was a charming person and a sport,
and the only human being except me that my
mother ever cared a hang about. His name
was Bargrave, Clyde Bargrave, and that's my
name too. They met at a dude ranch. Her
mother was going to break it up, so they ran
off to Mexico; he was in the money at the
time, I don't know why, but his luck changed
and he cleared out. She never did know what
became of him.

"Her mother was wild, of course; got her
to Europe, and got right in touch with the
faithful swain Cort Fenway. He behaved like
the gentleman he was, and I'll say this — it
seems to be a family of gentlemen. He knew
all about me, of course, and he helped with
money and visas, and I was smuggled into the

world without anybody being the wiser from that day to this — anybody who mattered, I mean. You can imagine that Mrs. Kane was only too glad to have my mother marry him in those circumstance — marry anybody!"

Gamadge asked: "What if Cort Fenway hadn't died, Mr. Bargrave?"

"Hadn't died?"

"What if he had survived his illness, and come back to France to find his child dead and illegally buried?"

"Oh — that wasn't more than a remote possibility; but my mother said he wouldn't have done anything. You don't know how he felt about her, but perhaps Mr. Blake Fenway will tell you. He wouldn't have allowed her to pass me off as Alden, naturally; but he'd have helped her conceal the circumstances of Alden's death. She would have told him that she hadn't been responsible at the time; out of her head with grief for Alden and worry about him. She wouldn't have told him that she had designs on the Fenway property. He'd have brought her home, and told people that Alden had died in France and was buried there. He'd have said that he knew all about it. Perfectly safe. In those post-war times nobody would have bothered to ask questions. He'd have adopted me, and I'd have been a member of the family. Please try to remember, sir, that what she did was only a technical misdemeanor. As for Mott's death, I'm really sorry; but he was an old man and useless, and he'd been a drag on you for years."

Fenway said: "You are not competent to judge the value I placed on my cousin; such values are not in your power of reckoning. I can't meet you on the common ground of ordinary human feeling. I can only ask you — since you will be able to understand that question, at least — what advantage it would have been to you to be confined in some institution for life? As you would have been, if Mr. Gamadge had not found the picture of Fenbrook."

"I had no choice, sir; from the moment Mrs. Grove decided to talk it was confinement in an institution or — well, what I face now. But my mother and I had plans for the future. I wasn't going to wait in an observation ward for an overhaul by specialists, you know; I would have escaped tonight. It wouldn't have been much of a job; Craddock and Thurley had convinced the police that I was an amiable child, and they were all awfully sorry for me and handling me with gloves. I had a place all ready to go to, and I wasn't afraid of being recognized. Would *you* recognize me?"

Receiving no answer, he went on: "Mother would have followed me as soon as she could walk, and settled near me. She had what money she'd saved, and she would have had more from you; a dam' sight better than nothing. I could have put in time with the armed forces, but that was all right; I had papers — I got them right here in New York. We should have been all right."

He paused, and his eye met Gamadge's. He said with a kind of malignant humor: "You were the one that ought to have been eliminated, but I thought that after Mott was dead you'd consult Mr. Fenway, and that he'd send you about your business. I didn't know you had another client in the house. But I had a queer sort of a hunch last night when I met you at the head of the stairs that you were ready for me, and so you were."

Gamadge said: "I'd like to ask you one more question, Mr. Bargrave."

"As many as you like."

"Only one: why have you obliged us with all this detail instead of putting up a fight?"

Bargrave looked very much taken aback. "Putting up a fight? What kind of a fight could I put up? If you mean Mott Fenway's death, what difference would that make in the outcome, since nobody could deny that I'd killed Mrs. Grove? And they told me upstairs that you'd found the picture, which contained proof that I wasn't Alden Fenway, wasn't therefore a half-wit, and *was* responsible. And how could I plead extenuating circumstances, or lack of premeditation, when you'd had Mrs. Grove's message and could check up on the trap at Fenbrook? She wouldn't tell you where the picture was; we knew well enough that she was saving the family scandal for Mr. Fenway alone; but she certainly told you her life had been threatened, and that there was a conspiracy. You must have the message, though how in the name of all that's wonderful she managed to write one and send it out —"

Gamadge said: "Nothing in any message I received from Mrs. Grove could be used against you in any court of law."

"No?"

"No."

Bargrave stood for a moment staring, too angry to speak. Then he pulled himself together. "It doesn't matter," he said. "I'd have had a long jail sentence, and I don't want that; I prefer to quit, as my mother did, or at least as soon as I can."

He swung away, but unfortunately for his poise he had at last forgotten the steel on his wrist. It brought him up short, and he was forced to stand tethered while the plainclothes man exchanged some words with Nordhall. Gamadge wondered whether those few minutes were not the bitterest that Mr.

Bargrave would ever know, since while they passed he could not even pretend to be doing as he chose.

But it was not long before he and his custodian were out of the room. The stenographer followed them. Blake Fenway sat looking at the empty doorway, and then put his head in his hands.

"A young fellow like that," he groaned, "condemned to such a life by his own mother!"

"From what I could make of him, sir," replied Gamadge, "it was the life he would have chosen for himself."

"I haven't" — Fenway raised his drawn face — "I haven't thanked you."

Gamadge could only answer that with a shake of the head. He went out into the hall, put on his hat and coat, and opened the door. He hated to face the street, for he knew what he would find there; Number 24 now belonged to the public. He thought that it would eventually be handed over to them, since no Fenway would ever live there now.

20

END PIECE

"Bargrave!" said Clara. "You know, it sounds like a made-up name to me."

"No doubt it was a made-up name." Gamadge lay almost flat on the chesterfield, doing his duty by his operatives with the help of a strong highball. Clara sat at his feet, Harold and Arline beside his sofa. The two last-named looked as tired as he did, but they wanted the story. "Mr. Clyde Bargrave senior," continued Gamadge, "was evidently not the kind of person who wishes to be tied down to bourgeois responsibilities by a permanent address. But he must have had charm; Mrs. Fenway doesn't seem to have resented his behavior in leaving her to her fate after the Mexican escapade."

"I hope Mr. Fenway will look after Craddock and Hilda Grove."

"Craddock will be kept on as secretary, I hope," said Gamadge. "To help Fenway with that memoir he wants to write about his family."

Arline exclaimed: "He won't want to write it now!"

"Won't he?" Gamadge turned his head to smile at her. "You don't know what the urge is, Arline, when once you've fallen under the enchantments of literature. That memoir will be the solace of Mr. Blake Fenway's declining years, and the view of old Fenbrook, reproduced in color, will serve as the frontispiece. Craddock and Hilda Grove will marry, and Craddock will be the luckiest man — next to me — on earth."

"I'm going to call," said Harold, "and explain about that accident. I never felt like such a fool in my life."

"It's funny," said Arline, "that Craddock was so fond of that Bargrave."

"Oh, he put up a wonderful show as Alden Fenway; born mountebank, I presume, like his accomplished father. But Mott Fenway and Caroline, being prejudiced, felt that there was something wrong about him. Craddock felt that there was something wrong, but — being prejudiced — thought the fault lay with Mrs. Grove. But they were all astray."

Harold said: "I am, still. How did you know your client was Mrs. Grove?"

"How did I know it?" Gamadge stared at him. "You really ask me that?"

"Certainly I ask you that. I don't know now

307

any more than I did yesterday, when I guessed wrong."

"You knew the client must be either Mrs. Fenway or Mrs. Grove, though."

"Because everybody else could communicate with the outside world. Nobody else would have had to throw a message out of a window."

"Neither could be in such a jam without the other knowing it," said Gamadge, "and neither could be kept in such a jam for a day by the other working alone."

"Oh."

"I was looking for the indispensable accomplice a few minutes after I entered the sitting room for the first time. That accomplice must be someone who could be on the spot twenty-four hours a day, for my client was — must be — watched day and night. I eliminated Blake Fenway, Mott Fenway and Caroline; they were by no means always on the spot. Craddock? His bedroom was on the top floor, and he seemed to come and go pretty freely. If only Alden Fenway had an adult brain, he and his mother could control Mrs. Grove as absolutely as if they had had her in a cell; as in fact they had, at night — I soon discovered that her room was between theirs, with no outlet to the hall.

"But the specialists had said that Alden

Fenway would never possess an adult brain. The inevitable question presented itself: *was* this young man Alden Fenway?

"If he wasn't, who could he be? A son of Mrs. Fenway's? If so an elder son, because though he might be more than twenty-five years old, he certainly couldn't be less. Mrs. Fenway's devotion to him and anxiety on his account were obvious; I thought he might be a son.

"Why should she perpetrate such a fraud? I remembered having been told that Cort Fenway had a life interest in half the Fenway property, and that after his death the principal would descend to his heirs. But if he died leaving no heirs? I supposed the principal would almost certainly not go to his widow, but would return to the family. That was the usual disposition of so large an estate, and to make it more probable in this case was my information that the elder Fenways had never much approved of their son's marriage.

"Mrs. Fenway's interest in the fraud, if fraud there had been, amounted to the difference between the income on several millions and whatever the family might allow her, or whatever her husband might have earned and saved. I did not think from what I had been told about Cort Fenway that the latter sum would be great.

"What had her opportunity been to commit this crime? She and Alden had been in Europe, Cort Fenway in this country when he died. If the boy had died first? I could only assume that he had died first, that his death had been concealed, and that a substitution had been made. Afterwards the history of this mother and son was buried in obscurity; they travelled, they were said to have consulted great specialists and stayed in sanatoria. But where were those specialists and sanatoria, where were their records now? And since his return to this country the supposed Alden had seen no specialists, no doctor but the family physician who had not laid eyes on Alden Fenway after that afflicted child was four years old.

"If I were right about the substitution, my client was in duress to two unscrupulous persons, one of them a strong and probably ruthless man. But in what kind of duress? Was she restrained by fear of immediate physical violence?

"I could not think that was all that restrained her. There were often many other persons in the sitting room, including a masseuse and a doctor; many opportunities to get a word to them and escape death. But what other kind of restraint could there be? The first arrow decided me on that point; Hilda Grove was at the other end of the telephone,

310

in a lonely house, and although she was not of Mrs. Grove's own blood, Mrs. Grove had cared enough about her to spend money on her education and maintenance; and Mrs. Grove's income, I gathered, had not been large. She might have been actuated solely by a sense of duty towards her husband's niece, but her dry reticence was no proof to me that she could not feel affection also.

"By the time she got her first message through to me there had been a deadlock between her and the others for almost ten days; they must keep her alive until she told them where the picture of Fenbrook was; she must keep silence, or — as she thought — Hilda would die. Meanwhile Bargrave hunted for the picture through the small hours of many nights, and Mrs. Fenway tried to soften her old school friend's obdurate heart. But the situation couldn't last forever; it must crumble whenever Hilda should be summoned away from Fenbrook. They had, as you know, planned for that desperate contingency; but they were not alone in having made a deadly plan — Mrs. Grove had got through to me.

"Not much good to her? That's what I thought when I looked at her there in the sitting room after she was dead. But she wouldn't speak before me, and I was waiting to lend a hand if necessary after Blake Fenway had the news. The trouble was that the heroic little creature had no fear for herself." He glanced at Harold. "It was thanks to you, Sergeant, that she had her moment of triumph and liberation at the end."

Harold said: "I wish I'd known this afternoon that Hilda wasn't meant to go down that shaft. I wasted a lot of sympathy. I wasted a lot of brainwork, too, wondering how and when the floors would be put back again afterwards without incriminating somebody."

"Incriminating Craddock," said Arline.

Harold ignored her. "The shaft was going to be left the way it was, with the knitting bag on the hook, to prove whatever they were going to say about Mrs. Grove?"

"Yes."

"No wonder there was something about the whole thing that made me feel sick."

Arline said: "You ought to have seen his face when he opened the front door up there. I thought first he was going to jump out at me and choke me to death."

"I thought you were somebody coming to ask Hilda to go look for that knitting bag."

Clara's face wore a slight frown. "Henry," she said, "when Mrs. Grove threw that first paper ball out of the window she didn't know a thing about you. The Fenways didn't expect you to call, they can't have talked about you much."

"No, my angel, they can't."

"Then how could she know that you'd understand her message, and somehow get into the house? How did she know you'd care?"

Gamadge smiled at her. "Blake Fenway said he had my books. Perhaps she'd read them."

"They wouldn't tell her all that!"

"Something of an author is supposed to get into his books, though. Perhaps mine told her that I always answer my letters."